CALEB

Alone in a Dangerous World, a Young Boy Grows to Manhood, Becoming a Force for Good

Eugene W. Vest

Dedication

I proudly dedicate this book to my wife, Nan, who encouraged me in my research and countless hours of writing, and who read and proof-read my work, and offered questions and suggestions that were immensely helpful.

Thank you, Nan.

Contents

ABOUT THE AUTHOR

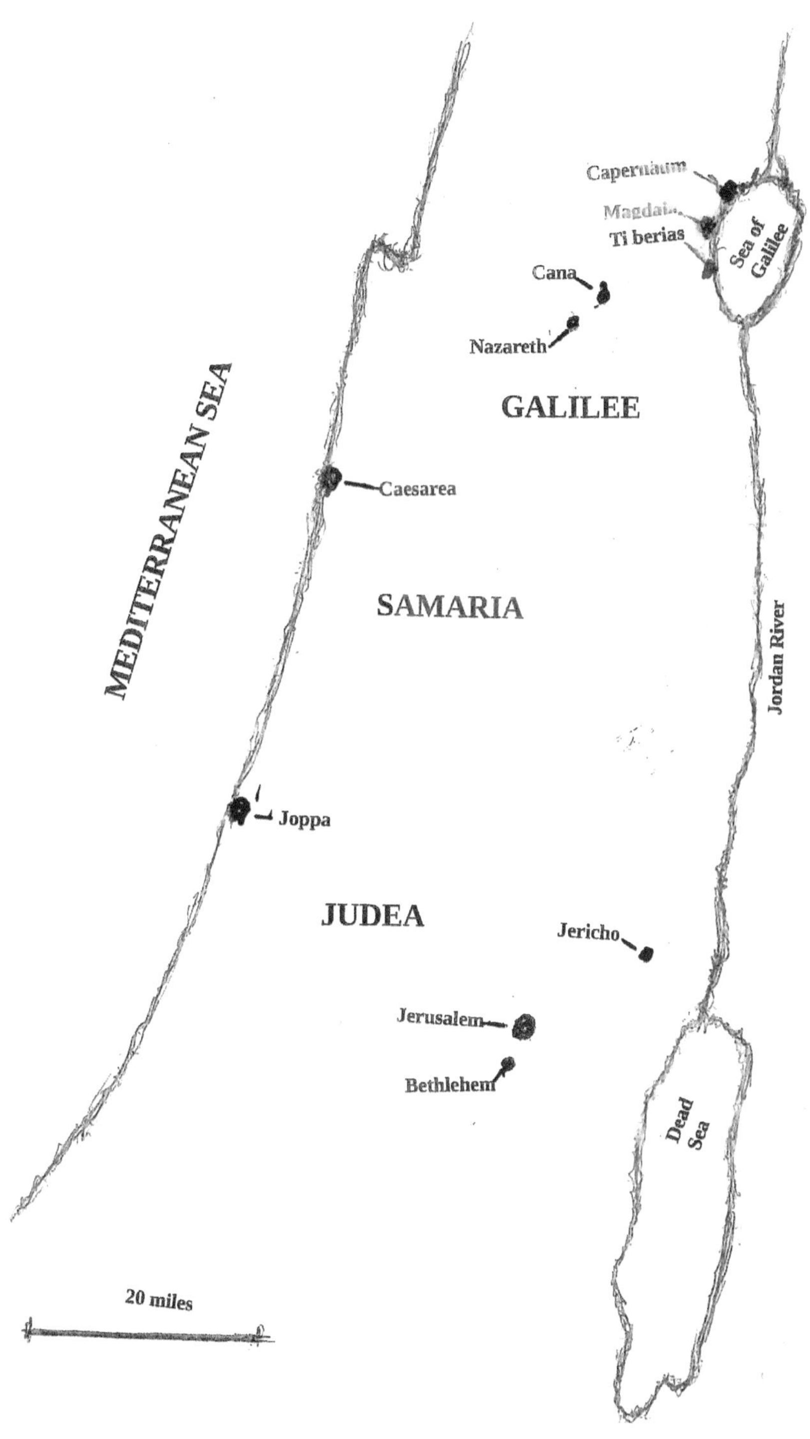

CALEB'S HOMELAND

Introduction

Over 2,000 years ago, Caleb, a Hebrew boy was born in the District of Galilee. At the age of twelve, he was separated from his parents and eight-year-old sister, and instantly became an orphan. He had no one to help him. Surviving many dangers, however, he grew to maturity in far-away Jerusalem. Then he heard of an unusual man back in Galilee, his birthplace, who could command events that were contrary to nature.

Caleb returned to his homeland to investigate these happenings. What he discovered only added to the mystery. But, as he gathered growing evidence, he reached an astounding conclusion.

CALEB

Alone in a Dangerous World,
a Young Boy Grows to Manhood,
Becoming a Force for Good

PART ONE

CALEB – THE BOY

This is Caleb's story – in his own words.

CHAPTER I
MOVE ON - OR DIE

LEAVING

I smell a lighted wick and notice a dim flickering image approaching our sleeping place. It is father, lighting his way with the oil lamp, the only lamp in our poor home.

Father sees that I am awake. He leans to my ear and whispers: "Get dressed. We're going on an adventure." Then he whispers the same to my sister, Ruth, on another cot. Ruthie is eight years old. I am twelve.

It is near midnight now. Rubbing our eyes, we dress, my sister and I. This is strange, but we do not question father. He snuffs the flame, and darkness returns. We put on day-clothes.

With our scant belongings, we silently leave our village home. We leave secretly, and quietly. I lead the family donkey. The few village huts have long gone dark. The night is solid black. We walk, picking our way carefully. For ages, it seems, we hear nothing but our shuffling footsteps. We stumble on. My little sister and I are puzzled. Is something wrong?

After a time, I notice the night air becoming cooler. A breeze is picking up. I hear, faintly, a distant sound. It grows louder and louder by the minute. Soon it's roaring. Violent winds are whipping us.

We are caught in it, a great storm. Father won't allow us to turn back. He yells above the roar: "Keep moving!" We hear but don't see. Too dark.

The wind is howling, and whipping, and threatening to throw us to the ground. I cannot even see the ground because of the pitch black night. Debris is flying through the air like weapons, and the wind beats us. We can't see, but we stumble on, sometimes briefly touching one another. Now I feel sprinkles, big ones. Rain crashes into us.

It pours, driven sideways by the wind, this way and that. Drops as hard as pebbles sting my face and hands. It must be the same for all of us, but I hear no cries above the storm. I vow not to slacken or give up. Lightning flashes, and thunder cracks and booms, over and over, with ear-splitting power. We push on.

In single file, father in front, me in the rear with our donkey, we stumble ahead, saying nothing. Our voices cannot be heard anyway. Father carries my little sister on his back, but I don't know how. We try to stay together, but the rain, the wind, and the black night make it near impossible; yet we do. The storm seems endless.

For hours, we slog through the brutal night, often stumbling, sometimes falling. Will it ever end? Yet, the wind and rain finally ease a little, as a hazy dawn emerges. Visibility is poor, but good enough to show that we are well beyond the sight of our village.

The storm is dying down to a drizzly wetness. The dirt trail has turned to mud, and scrubby plants everywhere are dripping the last of the rain. We still stumble because of roots and stones buried in the mud.

Exhausted, we stop walking. Father did not call a stop. But we do stop, unbidden, all of us, even the donkey. There is no place to sit down, just scrub brush and mud. We stand in shock, shivering. Mother tries to smile, but fails. Instead, tears slide down her cheeks. Ruth and I look at each other with questioning eyes.

Father draws flint and fluff from his kit to start a small fire with a few shavings. In spite of the wetness we feed the struggling flame with twigs and get it going. Finally it catches well. We hug the flames and try to quiet our quaking bodies. But soon father smothers the flames and we start anew. Our mood is somber. I hear stifled sobs.

Trudging along the muddy trail through scrub country, well off the travel path, I wonder: "Why, in Heaven's name, are we doing this?" But, still, none of us question father.

We are well off the public travel path in order to avoid travelers father says at last. We are dead tired. We've walked all night. The new day has blossomed. The sun has risen enough to comfort our bodies a tiny bit, but we find little to cheer us. Too tired.

I glance to the sky, now clear. Widely scattered vultures glide in lazy patterns. One or another will occasionally dip a wing for steerage or maybe a little boost.

While our scrub-country trail reduces chance encounters, it increases exposure to wolves, bears, wildcats, snakes, and scorpions. As night nears, our bodies and minds are totally spent in exhaustion. We search out dryer ground for sleep, wrapped in our thin robes. Its been maybe 20 hours since we left home.

Armed with heavy sticks, father and I take turns keeping watch by starlight. The night-air is chilly, but we make no fire. Too risky, father says. It could be seen for miles.

Morning brings no cheer, but we rise, stretch, eat and drink a little, ration out some oats to our donkey, and move on.

There are four of us, still walking, day after day, single-file. Five of us if you count Calli, our donkey. Besides mother, father, the donkey and me, there is my little sister, Ruthie. We are in the region of Galilee, heading south. This is the fourth day.

Father is leading the way, but I sense some uncertainty because of his troubled looks and frequent stops. He looks around, apparently for location. He and mother have a whispered conversation, and then we resume our trudging.

Ruthie grasps Calli's harness to keep from falling. As I said before, Ruthie is eight years old, and I am twelve, nearly thirteen. Ruthie doesn't smile anymore, not since we left our simple home now some four days ago.

Our home was in a wayside village of three others, basically huts, some half day's walk south of Nazareth. I say "was" because father told Ruthie and me that we would not be returning. He still calls this an "adventure."

Out of Ruthie's hearing, father adds a task for me: Be alert for possible pursuers. I'm proud that father shows confidence in me. I make sure now to follow at a distance behind the others, frequently looking back, and around, alert for unusual sights or sounds. If I notice any, I'm to run to father with the news. But I wonder: Why?

We walk on and on. Finally, on this fourth evening, at twilight, after we make a cold, dry, camp once again, mother whispers to me the reason we are fleeing. Fleeing!!? That means – danger!! Serious danger!! What is it?!! I listen carefully.

Mother speaks close to my ear to keep her message private. She says that father is being sought by agents of the tax collector, a hated person under contract to Rome. Rome occupies our land and extracts much of our wealth through taxation.

She tells me that father owes taxes that he cannot pay, and would be imprisoned if taken by the authorities. The rest of us would have no support and no income. We would likely fall into the lower caste of society, dependent on an uncertain charity to live.

Our tax collector is detested. He is unscrupulous, and he grossly overcharges. With little choice, father decided to take his family and flee. All of this I get from mother, in whispers.

Now I understand why we left our village with such stealth.

After a restless night, the fourth one of our flight, we're once again up and walking. It is the fifth day. With the hindrance of a slow, heavily loaded donkey, and eight-year-old Ruthie, we proceed slowly, still on the rough obscure trail, heading south. Father guesses that we are making maybe seven or eight miles each day, so now we may be about thirty miles from home. Well, it was "home," but not anymore.

Tiring on this hot dry day, the fifth, we stop briefly at mid-morning for a nibble of hard cheese and four swallows of water for each of us from our wine skin (now used only for water). Our food and water is rationed. During this brief rest, father takes me aside to confirm mother's comments about our fleeing. He says it's time that I should know.

He looks at me differently now, like a compatriot, leading our small poor family on a dangerous venture. He says we must keep the reason from Ruthie, though, for she might accidentally divulge it to our harm. Father and I now confer before making almost any decision. Any decision, that is, except … destination.

His mind, it turns out, is set on going to Jerusalem, some hundred miles from our former home. He tells this to us as we once again make a cold camp at the end of this day. He reckons that our journey may take us two or three weeks at our present pace.

Jerusalem is a large city, he tells us, as we settle in camp. Maybe fifty thousand people, or so (and many more at festival times). Some are street vendors, some religious people, some beggars, some wise men, and others of all sorts. He had been there, for some reason, as a young man. So he has a feel for the city from his own memory.

Jerusalem has a palace, a temple, synagogues, and all kinds of professionals (notably scribes, teachers, priests, and lawyers).

And the city is walled. Walled!!! Can you imagine!? In Jerusalem, we can assume a new identity and be free of the past. This is father's hope. I am so excited I can hardly sleep. I long for morning so we can move on.

We awaken to a clear morning. We are scruffy, and in need of a bath. But, not a chance.

The obscure scrub-country trail, that we're on, parallels the smoother public travel path, some two miles to our left. We are now beyond the likely range of people who know us, even on the public travel path. So father decides that we can risk the public path now, which will be easier walking.

We leave the scrub path and stumble along on rough rocky ground, with no path of any kind, for maybe a couple of miles, until we reach the public travel path. Once there, we turn south. Father is right, it is smoother and broader, and easier to walk on, but it has a lonely look. Though this path may be "public," I see no one, other than ourselves, in any direction. I think to myself, "we may as well be on the moon."

Finally, past noon, we come to a large lone boulder alongside the path which casts a shadow across our way. We stop and stand in the shade just for a moment's relief.

But as sudden as lightning, we're accosted by bandits. Three of them. They spring forth from behind the boulder and shove sacks over the heads and shoulders of mother and father. Father struggles mightily but cannot break free. The bandits seem very strong. They tie the hands of mother and father, then grab Ruthie. I am frozen by shock.

Father's yells are muffled by the sack, but they are shrill and unmistakable: "Run Kirby, run!" And again: "Run son, run, run!!" "Kirby, go!" ("Kirby was my given name at birth).

My feet fly as I shoot away for maybe a hundred yards before stopping to look back. One bandit is holding Ruthie, and the other two are restraining mother and father. Calli, the donkey, has skittered away, but I still see her, way down the travel path.

"Kirby" is the name father gave me at birth. He, himself, had been called that as a boy, and liked it, but, as an adult, he became known as Benjamin. This name lent dignity, he thought, and seemed to amplify his status as a wood carver (he fashions wooden dishes, spoons, and shallow bowls). This has been the basis of his/our income, but it has never amounted to much. In fact, we were always poor, too poor to keep up with taxes.

But, now, my mind is racing. I am only twelve (going on thirteen). I am now alone. I can expect no help. But I cannot be idle and expect to survive.

In the distance, I see my captive family being carried away on horses that must have been hidden nearby. They speed away through the wilds, vanishing in a fading cloud of dust. My eyes tear up, but I know that I must be brave. I remember father's urgent teaching while we camped, almost as though he had a premonition.

In evening camp of the last few days, father had tried to help me sharpen my wits, and to be alert to the evil intents of some people. He talked about robbers, liars, cheaters, deceivers, kidnappers, and slavery. He had said that one of the dangers of traveling by foot, alone or in small numbers, as we were, is that we could be captured by bandits and sold into slavery far away, where we were unknown.

"That's it!" It must be! The bandits could get no money because we have none, But they could sell mother, father, and Ruthie, as slaves. In some slight way, the thought heartened me. Their lives are too valuable for them to be murdered. Even if they are taken only one or two hundred miles away, they could be sold as slaves and probably never be discovered by old acquaintances.

As devastating as slavery may be, I feel some hope for their lives. I swallow my grief and turn my mind to my only choice: move on, or die. It will be dark before long. I try to settle down enough to think ahead. Tomorrow, I'll resume the march south as soon as possible. But, I wonder, will I make it to Jerusalem alive?

My first task before nightfall is to gather my thoughts and plan for tomorrow. I may have a couple of hours before total darkness. In that time, I must recover my donkey.

ALONE

The capture occurred just hours ago. It clouds my mind. This is still the same day, but it seems longer. I feel sick and weak. I need to eat, but have little food, and no appetite. I take a few deep breaths, determined to resist the thought of dying in this forsaken place. The land seems so vacant. There is a depressing silence, no sound but my own. I long for my stolen family. Yet, I know that I need to gather my wits and think carefully.

I must retrieve my donkey. I approach Calli slowly, speaking smoothly while edging toward her. Finally, she lets me come to her and take her lead line.

Next, I need to scout the area. With Calli in tow, I find a small hillock, climb up on it, stand straight, and turn slowly, scanning as far as I can see in all directions. No one. No sign of human life. I'm probably safe - for now.

Finally, I need to inventory the contents of the donkey pack. I must hurry. It will be dark within the hour. I remove the pack from my donkey's back and look inside. It smells musty. I remove the items, one by one.

Besides a little cheese, water, and oats, I find four things of possible value to me: a six-inch dagger and sheath, a few items of father's clothing (too big, but usable), and father's wood carving set (which I am not skilled to use, but may be able to sell). The fourth item is a small pouch containing five silver coins (each equal to about four day's pay). Mother's and Ruthie's few things are in the pack too, but of no use to me. I replace the pack's total contents except for the dagger and coins which I will carry.

I tether Calli to a small shrub and remove a little sleeping robe from the pack. I wrap up in the robe, lie down on my back, look up at the emerging stars, and say my prayers. Then, to my surprise, I break down in a flood of tears. Sobbing, I drift off to sleep.

I must have been very tired, for my next sensation is of Calli's stirring. I open my eyes. Dawn is breaking. I feel much better. I think the tears of last night did much to relieve the tension that gripped me yesterday. I lie still, in the warmth of my robe, just remembering my family.

My fingers touch the pendant that Ruthie gave me, maybe a year ago, when she was seven. It's Ruthie's star. I remember that day. Little Ruthie was so proud to be able to give me a gift. When she saw my pleasure, she was ecstatic. Ruthie had made the gift herself from a small piece of acacia wood that father had discarded from his work. It had the rough shape of a star.

I learned later that she had enlisted father's help in making a small hole in one of the star tips, from side to side, and then had gotten mother's help in finding a strong cord to thread through the hole. The cord, when tied at the ends, was long enough to go over my head and support the star on my chest. It seems weightless. To me, the star *is* "Ruthie." But, because mother and father had a hand in it too, it's my "family". I'll wear it always.

Refreshed after my sleep last night, I find that I'm thinking more clearly. To return home is out of the question because unpaid debts fall to the son if the father cannot be found. I suppose that makes me as much of a fugitive now as my father.

Therefore, I must "become" a different person to whomever I meet, whether friendly or hostile. I decide to abandon my given name and re-name myself "Caleb," and the family donkey, I re-name "Millie."

My best choice is to go south, toward Jerusalem as long as I am able. At this point, I rise from my musings, ready to face this new day.

I try to remember father's advice, sprinkled through my twelve years of life. His greatest teachings, though, began with this "adventure." Father told stories every night in camp, stories of deceitful and dangerous men. He hammered away on the importance of caution, especially in first encounters. Now his words come back to me: "Question motives, especially of strangers."

This looks to be a clear day. I give Millie a little water and grain, and re-load the robe and pack on her back. Millie and I have been together forever, it seems. Still, I know that someday, we may part.

I nibble some cheese and sip some water, and we set out on the travel path, Millie and I. No one is in sight in either direction, neither travelers nor wanderers. We head south.

Without thinking much, we walk on and on. I "talk" to my donkey as we stir the dust with each step. The sun is bright to my eyes, so I look mostly down to the pathway. We walk on. I cannot judge the distance we're covering.

But glancing ahead late in the day Millie and I notice a cluster of people and a few pack animals quite a way ahead. They are barely discernible. We stop where we are to study the group. They seem to be travelers, probably banded together for safety.

Moving closer, I see that they have stopped at a well where two or three locals seem to be in charge. Someone sees us and, with arm signals, motions for us to advance. We move ahead, cautiously.

Millie and I need water urgently, for ourselves, and for our water skin. But the attendants of the well, local men, demand payment, about one fourth the value of one of my coins. They

refuse to make change, and none of the travelers offer to help, so
I pay one of my silver coins in exchange for water for Millie and
me to drink, and to refill our water skin.

Cheated, I find no pity. But I neither cry nor sulk. I must appear
strong. Yet, I wonder if I'll survive. The travelers ignore me. I'm
among people, but I still feel alone.

MURDERER

Most of the travelers apparently know each other, but one seems
different, maybe a loner, like me, unknown to the rest. There's
a sinister look about him. Instantly, I do not like him. He makes
eye contact with me and edges to my side, looks at Millie and
says, "nice." I say, "thanks." He says his name is Ike. I tell him
that I'm Caleb. I try to break away from him.

But Ike follows me like a clinging vine. He asks, "Did you just
arrive? I don't remember seeing you when we assembled two
days ago in Caperneum."

One thing I know already: Ike is "bad news." He's too nosy, and
he looks strange, "mean" I should say. Oh yes, that's the look.
And now I remember to question his motives, just as father had
advised. I do this only in my mind.

To put him off, I say: "I've been trying to catch up, hoping to join
the group. I'm heading to Jerusalem to help my elderly uncle."
(not quite true)

Ike suddenly assumes the role of "adviser." He seems to want to
control me. He tells me that this group has a professional escort
for guidance and safety. At this point, Ike introduces me to Abe,
the escort, telling Abe that I am his friend. I shudder, inwardly.

Abe is armed with a sword, two daggers, bow and arrows, and a
horse which he sometimes rides, sometimes walks, leading him
by the halter. Abe is leading this group to Egypt, with a stop in

Jerusalem to let some drop out. He is willing to include me if the existing group unanimously agrees, but it will cost two silver coins. He works for hire, and won't make an exception.

With voice vote, the group accepts me and I relinquish two coins, leaving me with only two for myself. Abe thinks we'll be in Jerusalem in two days. For food, I'll live on my remaining stale cheese and water. It's now late in the day, so I expect Abe will have us all sleep in the open tonight.

Ike, who is still trying to befriend me (or perhaps ensnare me), tells me that he is glad that I joined up. He has some dried dates, and offers me a couple. I know that they will be good for me, so I accept. But I wonder why he is interested in me. I can't help being suspicious.

I notice that the other travelers do not interact with Ike…. nor with me, for that matter. He has a surly, dark, disposition, which he tries to mask with an unconvincing smile when close to me.

His features are craggy to start with, and his voice is gravelly and deep as though seasoned by years of drink and hard living. And he wears an eyepatch over his left eye, and his right hand is missing.

Has Ike been punished? Or had an accident? Is he an escaped convict? A wanted man? Or just down on his luck? He looks to be maybe forty years old, but it's hard to tell.

Waiting my turn at the wash basin on this, my first evening with the group, I catch him stealing. It happened quickly.

One of the group who was washing some sticky gooey substance from his hands, had placed a gold ring on a nearby flat rock. I suppose this made it possible for him to clean up better. When he turned to pick up his ring, it was gone. The traveler sent up a yell, calling for his ring, but no one admitted seeing it.

Being a newcomer to the group, I had been standing quietly,

26

waiting to be the last to wash up. While I was eyeing everyone, trying to size up the group, I saw the ring disappear from the rock. Ike had just walked casually by the rock. He did not stop, but I glimpsed his one hand pass near the rock and scoop up the ring with such a fluid motion that the theft was not seen by anyone but me.

Being basically honest, and naive perhaps, I approach the wretched Ike in private, and tell him that I saw what happened. I urge him to return the ring. He denies that he has the ring. Even so, he says, if I accuse him publicly, he will have to kill me. He bends to my ear and whispers hoarsely: "I've killed men before. One more won't matter."

Ike has put a deathly fear into me. I decide to avoid him as much as possible, and to resist any attempt by him to cultivate an attachment to me. I check the dagger under my tunic. I stick close to Millie, and give her a lot of attention in order to seem busy.

Abe, our escort, organizes a search of the grounds encircling the wash stand, assuming his client's ring has been accidentally knocked from the rock. Six of the younger men with keen eyesight comb the grounds, inch by inch. An hour later, they report no success. The client accepts the conclusion that his lost ring will not be recovered. The possibility that it was stolen never comes up, but I notice people checking their valuables and seeming more alert.

The sun is sinking. It will soon be dark. Abe builds a small open fire, and we all settle down for the night. Lodging is not available, so we'll sleep under the stars. I remove Millie's pack, tie her lead to my wrist, and use the pack for a pillow. I'm determined to stay awake, but, in spite of myself, I drift into restless sleep.

Around midnight, I awake with a start. A footstep on gravel alerts me. I do not move, but open my eyes wide. A figure is tiptoeing away from the clustered group. He raises a hand to the watchman, who returns the recognition. It's Ike, going to relieve himself, probably. He soon returns to his sleeping spot and settles in. I saw nothing amiss, but I did notice that he walked with a stoop, with his one hand close to the ground. Once again, no matter how much I try to stay awake, I drift to sleep.

At last, I sense the coming dawn. Creatures begin to stir. A rooster from the village that owns the well loudly signals a new day. And I hear telltale sounds of goats and sheep. Wild dogs are howling in the distance, and the screech of a soaring eagle splits the air.

I rub my eyes and nibble some cheese and am about to eat the second date I had saved from yesterday. While chewing the date, I tend to Millie and re-load my pack on her back, along with my sleeping-robe. Others are rising and stretching.

Abe, our escort, is suited up, has given his horse oats and water, and is now checking on the health and readiness of his group. There are 19 of us, now that I've joined them. We're all on foot except for Abe who sometimes rides on ahead, but never out of sight, scouting for bandits or natural obstacles.

Abe tells me that we should reach Jerusalem tomorrow before sundown. Ike, the murderer (he admitted it to me), is trying to renew our contact of yesterday but I am uneasy. I direct my attention to Millie.

We set out, moving at a good clip. Abe frequently scouts ahead, and often takes a headcount and inquires of our well being. He is a good escort. We walk on, almost without thinking, for hours.

Walking is monotonous. We are all tiring and glad to stop, even briefly, for a noontime break. We approach another small village with a public well. This well is attended by locals to avoid overuse but, unlike the one of yesterday, they do not charge. I can clearly see that God has blessed me because I am down to my last two silver pieces.

The sinister Ike revives my caution when he asks me if he can do anything for me. I say, "no thanks," maybe a little curtly, and he backs off, but not much. I sense that being alone, though in a group, makes me vulnerable to most any kind of evil, so I resolve to be as alert as possible and trust my senses.

Mother (I so miss her) would have said "trust God to care for you," and I do, but I intend to use all the abilities God has given me. I am watchful.

Once again, Ike comes along side of me as we resume walking. He says in a low voice: "Caleb, I think you're lying. I think you're a run-away, and don't really have a needy uncle in Jerusalem. What do you say to that?" I say: "That's crazy, man! I don't know how you came up with such a wrong idea. I tell you, my uncle is waiting for me in Jerusalem" (untrue). "Now drop it." (tough talk from a twelve year old).

After a pause, Ike says: "We can be a great team, partners, you and me. Think about it, Caleb. In Jerusalem, we can get rich. You draw attention while I rob them. They will never catch us." We continue in silence until nearly dusk when we come to a stop for this day. I detest Ike, and fear him more than anyone I've ever known.

Finally, with the sun setting, we all bed down (I with Millie's lead again tied to my wrist) for this final night before reaching Jerusalem. I don't know what my next move may be, but I intend to enter the city alone tomorrow, somehow.

Abe had confirmed just before dark those of us who would break off at Jerusalem; there would be eleven of us, including Ike (the rest are going on to Egypt). I'm lying on my back, looking at the stars, and wondering how I will break away from Ike. He persists in trying to entice me as a "partner in crime" of some sort. I've got to get away.

I hope to blend into Jerusalem as a loner looking to settle down. My immediate objectives are to ditch Ike, gain anonymity, and find an honest way to live. I have two pieces of silver and a donkey. I may need to sell my donkey, and ... I need to lose Ike.

I must have slept like a log, for suddenly (so it seems) it is morning and Abe is doing a head count. Each of us does his or her morning routine (three women are traveling with us). There is considerable excitement among those of us dropping out at Jerusalem.

Abe will guide us to a travelers' station within the city walls where he will pick up additional travelers for the continued trip to Egypt. We're plodding along at a steady pace when we are startled from our thoughts by someone yelling: "City walls!!, just ahead!!" Another cries: "There it is!" And, sure enough, I see it too!

A fog of grief nearly overcomes me as I think of father, mother, and Ruthie. This is where father wanted to be. I breathe a quick silent prayer for their safety, and wonder if they are alive. I shake the feeling with difficulty, and search for a moment when I may steal away from all the group, including, Ike - especially Ike. We move on.

The North Gate is just ahead. Important people are mingling with each other just inside the gate. Someone says they are "elites," some of the wise men of means, gathered, as they frequently do to socialize, and maybe cultivate business deals.

A short stone's throw beyond the "elites," sit a cluster of beggars looking sad and dirty. I learn these designations from the chatter within my travel group; otherwise, I would have no idea. Thus begins my learning of Jerusalem life, and even though I am very young, it dawns on me that I must learn the ways of this city, and learn them entirely on my own.

I have neither a tutor, mentor, nor family, to help me. A sense of helplessness nearly sinks my will to live, but I shake it off knowing that I must act somehow, or die. I cannot allow myself to sit down by the street and weep. I am still in the group but not for long because we are approaching the group's reassembly station.

Four impressively uniformed Roman soldiers, on horseback, are awaiting us. Abe says this is unusual. He orders us to leave the talking to him unless any one of us is directly questioned by a soldier. Our group instinctively tightens. I notice Ike near the edge of the group. He has snatched off his eyepatch, revealing an ugly dripping cavity.

The captain of the soldiers greets us, then orders us to stay close together. He says he and his comrades intend to visually inspect and interrogate each of us, one at a time.

He informs us that a murderer has escaped from a Capernaum jail, up north, on the Galilean Sea. He asks Abe if he might have noticed any suspicious behavior among his charges. Abe declares no such notice, and assures the captain that his group is fully intact. No one has left.

The Roman captain orders each of us to come forward, one at a time, when called, stand before the soldiers, and answer the captain's questions. First, he orders the three women to come forward and stand together, but apart from the others; this because he is searching for a man. The women are exempt.

Next, he describes the features of the man he is hunting: eyepatch (probably), hoarse or gravelly voice, missing right hand, about forty years old. At this, Ike tears away and darts into the nearest side street, into a home, and out of sight.

The three subordinate soldiers, still mounted, charge into the street, but since Ike had disappeared into a home, the soldiers had to dismount, leaving one to keep the horses while the other two burst into the home – but – too late.

Ike had fled through the back of the dwelling, into a courtyard, then into another home, and out the front into yet another side street, and now was nowhere to be seen. Ike had eluded his would-be captors. But, he is now a marked man within the city of Jerusalem.

The city gates are watched, and the walls are patrolled, so Ike is effectively contained somewhere in the city. He will probably be captured someday, but in the meantime, he is a murderer at large, and a danger to everyone, including me.

The Roman captain apologizes for the disruption and assures everyone that the escapee will be caught soon (I am dubious about the "soon" part). I feel a shiver of fear, knowing that I will have no more solid footing in Jerusalem than Ike does, and we will both be roaming, but for different reasons.

Abe and the captain bid each other goodbye, and the travel group re-settles. Abe separates those continuing to Egypt from the rest of us, and collects the new additions to the group for the continued journey. Abe extends well-wishes to those staying, and turns his attention to the others.

I say goodbye to no-one, but take Millie by her lead and head down a narrow side street in a direction opposite to that taken by Ike. I move briskly to look like I know where I'm going, hoping to avoid any suspicions among the few lingering travelers. It is dusk. Darkness is only minutes away.

The street I'm on just now is lined with small dwellings. Most have a little garden, and a shed for a few animals. I notice goats and chickens. There may be more, but darkness envelops everything now and I cannot discern much beyond my next step. However, I did sense what seemed to be a grape arbor beside the street, so I felt around blindly until my hand found grapes. I snap a bunch off, hoping they are ripe (I know this is stealing). They prove to be good enough so I eat them, slowly, one by one.

Wow!! Fresh fruit! The first since our stealthy departure from our former tiny village nearly two weeks back.

Then, thanks be to God, in the darkness I nearly tripped over something. Feeling around, as a blind man, I discovered that it was the low wall of a public well. So Millie and I stopped and quenched our thirst to the fullest, at last.

Restored a bit, Millie and I lay down near the well - totally exhausted. With her lead tied to my wrist once again, we fall asleep … as I wonder where the murderer is.

REUBEN

Awakening to a strange sound, a soft rumble and a rhythmic shuffle, I'm instantly alert, eyes wide, ears sharp, but I don't budge. Could it be Ike?

It's not yet day. There is only the slightest hint of the coming dawn, a barely perceptible easing of the inky sky far above the still-dark street on which I lay. Only the brightest stars still sparkle. Their weaker sisters await another night. My donkey lies quietly at my side, perhaps still sleeping.

A man is slowly approaching through the near-black shadows, pulling a sizable cart toward the well where Millie and I lay. I'm about to flee; that is, until I sense that the man is a worker, intent on his chore, and probably not concerned about me. He is clearly not Ike, the murderer.

My donkey stirs a little as I prop up on my elbows for a better look. I judge the cart to be around four feet wide and six feet long. It has wooden sides standing up about a foot. As the darkness of night begins to fade, I see more detail. The cart has two slim parallel poles extending forward with the worker walking between them, and with his hands on the poles, one on each.

A leather harness, attached to the front of the cart, is wrapped around the worker's shoulders and around his chest. He apparently supplies the pulling power with his body, and steers with the two parallel poles. He is looking down, minding his steps, but when he is nearly upon Millie and me, he looks up with a start, surprised to see us. He stops in his tracks.

After an awkward silence while we take the measure of each other, he says "shalom." I reply with the same greeting. Looking at Millie and me, he asks: "*Are you OK?*" I assure him that we are fine, just tired from traveling, and having no one to call on, we simply lay down at this well for a rest, and fell asleep.

Presently, he asks, "*Where are you from?*" I say: "The Province of Samaria." (untrue because my former home was in the Province of Galilee, just north of Samaria - but I want to erase my past). I'm thinking now that this cart man may be lacking, mentally. His first two comments were uttered in a halting voice, and he had paused a moment, seemingly to formulate his next thought before speaking again.

Then, slowing my own pace of speech, I said: "I am a young man (sounds better than "boy" in this case), striking out on my own. My hope is to learn the ways of Jerusalem because this is where I want to live. By the way, my name is Caleb." The cart man, after a lingering pause, said: "*My name is Reuben.*" Reuben smiles. His smile is a little lop-sided, but with a certain charm.

Reuben has considerable facial hair, but it is neatly trimmed. He looks to be around twenty years old, eight or ten years older than I. I wonder if someone trims his beard for him, and maybe even guides him in his personal cleanliness and general appearance because he has a neatness about him.

He is wearing a typical tunic for a working man, falling just below the knees, like mine, but his is cleaner. My own tunic has become soiled from travel, and my sleeping in it.

I ask Reuben what he's doing, and he tells me, haltingly, that he is the stable man for his father, and he is now here to collect water for the animals. It develops that his father, whose name is Dan, owns a commercial stable service, where he keeps several donkeys, three or four mules, one team of horses, and three teams of oxen.

Dan's animals are available, by rent or lease, to qualified

teamsters or donkey masters. Dan also provides boarding service for animals of owners who lack space of their own. And he is a broker, buying and selling animals on behalf of others. To top it all, Dan is an animal doctor.

I learn all this from Reuben while I help him fill a dozen clay jars with water from the well (this is for the animals at the stable). I judge that the loaded cart will require a great deal of strength to move it, and **strength** seems to be abundant in Reuben's body. He clearly stands a good six feet in height, is broad shouldered, muscular, and healthy. His color is good, a little dark, but that seems to be his nature.

Reuben possesses a certain innocence though, and it shows when he tells me about a couple of bullies who like to loiter between the well and his father's stable. They taunt Reuben, pepper him with gravels, call him an ass, or worse. Reuben takes it, he says, even though tears sometimes slide down his cheeks.

In the rapport that is budding between us in this short time, Reuben reveals this bullying issue to me, and I am touched by his confidence. Presently, he says: *"I could hurt them bad, but I don't, because I can't hurt anything with life in it, not even a bug."*

I'm thinking about my new friend now. He seems so different, so rare as a person. After while, he speaks again. *"God makes life."* Then he falls silent, turns to the cart, re-harnesses himself, and takes his position between the guide poles, and with a mighty heave, starts the rig rolling. Over his shoulder, he says: *"Come, I'll show you my animals."* So Millie and I join him.

The sun is emerging above the roof-tops now, so we have much better light.

I can't believe how quickly I'm coming to appreciate Reuben. We're heading slowly to his stable. I have Millie by her lead, and Reuben and I are making our way in happy quiet companionship.

But at this moment, I see two boys ahead, just standing in the street as though waiting for Reuben, and now, Millie and me as well. We are now within a few feet of them. Trying to look hostile, they stand in the lane and threaten our passage. I tie Millie's lead to the cart and step forward, ahead of Reuben.

I ask the boys to step aside, but they snarl and try to look menacing. Now, I am tall for a twelve year old, maybe half a head shorter than Reuben. I have never been in a knife fight, but I impulsively draw my dagger (once father's) from my tunic just far enough for the boys to see the hilt and about an inch of blade, and I order them to step aside.

Thankfully, they do step aside and watch quietly as we pass by. The boys saw the dagger, but Reuben did not, and I did not tell him.

Now at the stable-yard, I open the gate for Reuben and he passes from the street into the yard, and on into the stable itself. Millie and I follow. I close the gate securely. The stable is clean. It smells of a pleasant combination of animals, hay, and grain. There is a loft with a good supply of hay, and, down below, bins for grain. While I watch, Reuben refills the animal's shared water tank in the center of the stable yard, and distributes measured amounts of hay and grain in each occupied stall.

Each animal has its own stall, all of which have a feed trough at the head end. Each stall is open at the rear to allow the animals to back out to go to the common wooden water tank.

Between the stable and the street, the small exercise yard for the animals is fenced to keep them from wandering into the street. The street is lined mostly with dwellings. To the rear of the stable, away from the street, another fenced enclosure exists as a training area where animals are worked at training tasks to keep them familiar with commands, harnesses, and typical work.

Reuben proudly introduces me to each animal, and assigns a spare stall to Millie. I remove Millie's pack and hang it on the wall of the stall. Then Reuben, who seems to have taken to me, insists on having me meet his family. I'm a little nervous about this, but see little choice.

At the kitchen door, Reuben removes his sandals. He looks at my feet which are still bare (my sandals are in the donkey pack) and motions me to come on in anyway.

Breakfast aroma fills the air. This is my first impression. I see porridge, steaming hot, and some kind of bread unlike what I've seen before. And, of course, there is Reuben's parents, seated at the table. Reuben introduces me in his halting way. I bow and say: "Shalom." Dan returns the greeting with a smile. Reuben's mother smiles but does not speak.

 "Reuben met me at the well," I say, "and has been very kind to me. I hope I'm not intruding." "Not at all," says Dan. "Come and have some porridge with us, and we can talk. This is my wife, Leah." So, we eat, and talk, and begin to get acquainted.

Reuben excitedly begins in his struggling way to tell of our meeting, and that I had helped him fill his water jars, and had walked back to the stables with him, and, most amazing of all to him, that I had told the mocking boys to step aside, and they did.

His parents knew that Reuben was sometimes pestered with insults and showers of pebbles, but they also knew that Ruben always, without fail, completed his chores. The difference, now, is that Reuben seems so happy that I had taken up for him. That makes a great impression on Dan and his wife, and at that, they become even friendlier and ask me to stay for the day.

Dan asks me to tell them how I came to be where Reuben found me, and with a donkey, no less. I decide to tell the truth – mostly – but not my original home location, nor the real reason my family was traveling (just in case I'm being sought for father's delinquent taxes).

I begin my account, saying: "Father wanted to come here, to

Jerusalem where he hoped to profit from his skill as a wood carver, carving wooden dishes, bowls, spoons, ladles, and spits, for sale to the people here.

Our little village is quite small. It has no name. It's somewhere in upper Samaria, but I am unable to pinpoint the exact location. We are poor. We could not afford to join an escorted travel group, so we struck out as a family of four and a donkey, alone. There was father, mother, sister Ruthie, me, and the donkey.

"On our way, we were attacked by bandits who made off with all but me and the donkey. As father struggled, he yelled for me to run, and run fast. Not knowing what else to do, and even though I was in shock, I managed to avoid capture and retrieve the donkey. I continued on until I came upon an escorted travel group heading for Jerusalem and beyond.

"The group took me in for a small fee which I was barely able to meet with coins I had found in the donkey pack. It was enough for one person and a donkey, but would not have been enough for our family of four. I guess that's why father never joined us to an escorted travel group.

The group that took me in dropped me and a few others here yesterday. The group reformed and is continuing on to Egypt, and is probably back on the travel path today. I stumbled upon your public well just after dark last night, sat down, and fell asleep. The well is where God blessed me with the appearance of Reuben this morning."

Dan and Leah just look at me and say nothing. I wonder if they believe such an improbable story. After a time of silence, Dan clears his throat and says: "You've had a horrible experience. Do you have any idea where your family may have been taken?" "No," I say, "but they are healthy and strong. I can only wonder if they are to be sold as slaves." I'm stifling my emotions now, trying to not break down.

Silence fell upon us as Leah picked up the dishes. Finally,

Dan presented a list of chores for Reuben to do this day: two deliveries of rental donkeys this morning, and a trip beyond the city walls this afternoon to gather as much scrap firewood as he can find in the rough countryside. Reuben, in his halting way, and somewhat timidly, asked: *"Father, would it be OK for Caleb to go with me today?"*

Dan looks at me and says: "Maybe Caleb has other plans … but, if not, why not take him along and start acquainting him with the city." Then, his eyes turn to me as he asks if I would like to go along and maybe give Reuben a hand here and there.

I jump at the chance, thank my hosts for the wonderful breakfast, and as Reuben and I head for the door, Dan calls out: "And come back for supper, and stay the night with us. We'll put an extra sleeping pallet on Reuben's bedroom floor for you! And don't forget to feed your donkey from the stable supplies. No charge!" Dan is chuckling, and Leah is smiling as Reuben and I head out.

JERUSALEM

Breakfast over, Reuben and I return to the stable and find the animals standing or meandering in the exercise yard between the stable and the street. Having been fed and watered before our own breakfast, they are relaxed and gentle. Reuben begins picking suitable donkeys for the renters.

One donkey is older and very gentle, He selects her for the first renter, he says, because the renter is hosting a party, and wants to give his children and visiting cousins rides. He wants a cart too, for the tots who are too young to ride the donkey but can still enjoy cart rides. The second customer also needs a cart for transporting furniture.

Reuben and I set out with the two donkeys, each equipped with a cart, and travel about a quarter mile through the city streets to reach the first renter's home. I pay close attention to the streets, noting the street direction and anything special that might help me when I may some day be on the streets alone. We visit for a while with the renter and some of his family, and make the handover of the animal and cart as easy as possible, answering any questions as to the care and handling of the donkey.

Completing this delivery, we cross several streets before turning south. We finally reach the home of Jacob, an older man. Jacob's task for the day is to move furniture for his daughter who is moving from Jacob's home to another where she and her new husband are taking up residence. This delivery goes as smoothly as the first, and we head home. I say "home," but, really, I'm only invited for one night!).

Now we're walking on a street parallel to the inner side of the city wall when we approach a principal city gate (I must learn the name of the gates) which we will pass by, but not go through.

People are sitting along the street just inside the city gate, maybe a dozen or so of them. Reuben says that they are beggars, pleading for alms from well-to-do persons entering the city.

In so many words, he says the beggars have a noticeable hierarchy in their seating positions (he is a better observer than I would have imagined). Reuben says that the beggars closest to the street seem to be the most fit, and they reappear in the same seating position every day. Newcomers and weaker persons are forced to the rear.

Travelers toss coins to them. Most land close to the nearest beggars, but a few coins make it all the way to the rear. Scrambling for coins in the rear section is rough and competitive because so few coins reach them.

SUDDENLY, A JOLT! I see a back-row beggar with an eyepatch! He is mostly covered with what appears to be a cast-off robe, dirty and tattered. Travelers have just now tossed some coins, and I see the one-eyed beggar scramble for a coin with one hand, rather than two like the rest.

No question! He's the escaped murderer! I know! And the man

spots me walking with Reuben. This man fears only one person – me! -- because I know who he is, and can turn him in. THE MAN IS IKE! Now I must be ever cautious and alert. Ike may try to kill me, but, at least, I have a better idea of where he is.

Reuben does not know that Ike and I have just recognized each other. I maintain the steady pace set by my new friend. We continue on toward the stable. Reuben is telling me about Jerusalem. In so doing, he informs me that his father's home and business is in the poorest district of the city.

Dan is probably the best-off of the poor because of his business. His animal business makes him fairly well known city-wide, though not a social equal with the wealthy. Reuben tells me that everyone likes his father, and his mother too. I can see that he is proud of them.

I'm discovering that Reuben is a man of quality and not slow-witted at all. In fact, he's quite bright. I like Reuben. I hope we have a growing and lasting friendship.

I ask Reuben if he knows where the beggars go for the night, and where and how they get food. He says that they slip into sheds and stables, or any other shelter not occupied or normally visited by their owners after dark.

His father found a beggar in the hay loft of their stable one morning when he had gone early to check on a sick mule. The beggar was frightened by the discovery, tried to escape but was blocked by Reuben's father. His father gave the beggar some bread and warned him not to come to the stable again because, for one thing, it disturbs the animals. It also packs down the hay by sleeping on it, making it less fresh for the stock.

Reuben further said that beggars either beg or steal food, or use some of their gifted coins to buy food in the marketplace. He says the beggars are generally tolerated, but not welcomed as companions. I feel that I'm learning more about Jerusalem by the hour.

At the stable, Reuben drinks a mix of water and wine, and eats a small piece of bread which Leah had left for him as usual. She had, this day, left the same for me. Gratefully, I eat the bread and drink only the water. I do not drink wine or any fermented drink by choice, but I mean to thank Leah just the same.

Reuben and I sit and talk for a bit, mostly about Jerusalem. Then we hitch another donkey to a cart in preparation for our firewood search. We leave the city by the Dung Gate. This opens to a dried out valley where dead shrubs and broken tree limbs, having fallen from weak or dead trees, litter the ground.

I see at least two other searchers in the area. One is an old woman, tying dried twigs in a bundle, to carry home on her back. Reuben and I encounter two snakes and a scorpion as we work. It takes most of the afternoon to fill the cart, but, finally, we do, and head for home. At home, we unload the wood and place it in neat bins, sorted by twigs for starters or small fires, and bigger pieces for longer fires.

The evening dinner is a delicious lamb stew. The family, including me, for this evening at least, linger over the meal and discuss our day. Dan treated two sick animals outside the city today. Leah baked more bread and prepared the lamb stew. Reuben and I review our full day too. And, we all talk until dusk, when Leah tidies up the kitchen before we all go to our sleeping quarters. Reuben and I sleep on mats on the floor of his room.

Morning brings the aroma of fresh bread, porridge and fruit to my nostrils. Reuben is stirring. Leah is humming in the kitchen. We soon gather for breakfast. Dan recites a blessing, and we begin to eat.

Dan pauses in his eating, looks at me, and smiles. So does Leah. I pause too, expecting something, but having no idea what. Then he says: "Leah and I have noticed that you and Reuben work well together." "Yes," I say, "and I'm learning a lot from him too. He is a good teacher." Dan and Leah show sure signs of pleasure at that. Reuben has not received much praise from anyone except his parents in all his years.

Then, the most wonderful thing! Dan invites me to stay with them for as long as I want, at least until I learn the ways of Jerusalem, or until I find more profitable employment. I can hardly believe my ears! Two days ago, I was a dirty, weary wretch, sleeping in the open at the local well, and now I'm invited to be a part of this poor but wonderful household.

Dan says that he cannot pay much, maybe one silver coin a month, plus room and board, and feed and shelter for my donkey. I quickly accept, hugging all of them, bowing and thanking them earnestly for this privilege. It's a joyful time.

As the glee subsides a bit, Dan assigns a rather complicated errand to Reuben and me. It may take most of the day, and it looks like a rainy day at that. Not pleasant.

The weather is wet and foggy (a rare condition) and the streets are muddy. Visibility is limited. Reuben and I are walking in this terrible weather on our assigned errand. We are passing a dwelling when Ike, who was lurking on the hidden side of it, springs from the corner with a dagger aimed at my gut. Reuben and I jump in startled surprise.

Ike thrusts his dagger at me in slashing sweeps, over and over, but misses every time due to my quick reaction. Reuben (who would not kill a bug - remember?), throws his massive body at Ike, pinning his ugly frame to the muddy street, face down. Ike's dagger flies from his hand to the muddy street, and I grab it. Reuben is rubbing Ike's face in the mud, but finally lets him up. Ike rubs mud from his one good eye and darts down a side street and disappears.

Reuben surprised himself by his defensive reaction, his instinctive use of force. We talk about this for a bit while our heartbeats slow down, restoring a measure of calm to us. Reuben was apologetic about harming our attacker, but he's beginning to feel better, I notice, as I praise him. Finally we resume our original task with no further trouble. Reuben is clearly a "new man," and, I notice, very protective of me.

Finally, at home, with his mother and father and me, he reviews his heroism with a bit of pride that I had not seen before. Dan and Leah listen intently. And they clearly show a heightened pride in their big son. We give Ike's dagger to Dan for safe keeping. They do not know that I carry a dagger of my own.

Dan, Leah, and Reuben, apparently assume that the attack on Reuben and me was a random act committed by a desperate thief. It does not occur to them that I may have been targeted, specifically. They do not know of Ike. And I do not tell them.

By and large, my life with Dan, Leah, and Reuben is peaceful and pleasant, and over time, it becomes routine, day to day. There are only minor variations from one day to the next. Reuben and I are happy companions, co-workers, and very solid friends.

Days pass, then the months and the years: swish - swish - swish - year in, year out. I lose track of time, except that I know that I was born soon after Passover, so I take note of each Passover and add a year to my age, plus twelve, my age when I lost my family. By that reckoning, I am now twenty years old. I have few concerns . . . only to watch for Ike.

PART TWO

CALEB – THE MAN

CHAPTER II
EIGHT YEARS LATER

DEATH

Wow!! Eight years!! How fast they passed!! How quickly, it seems, that I grew from a boy of twelve to a strong healthy man of twenty.

After eight years in Jerusalem, I've become familiar with all the streets, all major buildings including the Temple, all other public and official buildings, and many of the people and where they live. My only concern is Ike, a murderer and a beggar, a continuing threat to me. I spot him occasionally among the beggars.

Other than that, life is easy. I don't know why, but it seems too good to be true.

This morning, Reuben and I water and feed the animals as usual before going back to the house for breakfast. While we eat, Dan discusses the job for today, and says he will need the help of both Reuben and me all day. Reuben and I are to get oxen and equipment ready and take it all to a new work site just outside the city. Dan will join us later to begin the job, which is to plow a field for a long-time customer.

As soon as Reuben and I finish breakfast, we set to work. First, we yoke a team of oxen. Then we hitch the team to a cart on which we load a plow, harrow, and a drag. We set out to the work site figuring it will take an hour to get there because the oxen move slowly. Reuben walks with the oxen, guiding them, while I sit in the cart to steady the implements.

We're soon approaching the city gate through which we'll pass, but there is some commotion blocking the passage. Not knowing what it is, Reuben halts the oxen while I jump out of the cart to race ahead. I'm there in seconds. A crew of city workmen are doing something, but I don't know what. They have a cart and donkey rig stopped in the gateway. Men are milling about in excited conversation, judging by their motions.

Now I see it. Two men with a litter are carrying a corpse. They're going from the nearby beggar place to the cart. An arm dangles from the litter. It's hand is missing. I push my way closer and see that this is **Ike**, the murderer. After all these years! Eight years! Can you believe it? It is **Ike,** for sure. They will probably bury him in the paupers' field, a short walk beyond the gate.

I hand a coin to one of the gawking beggars, and ask what happened. The beggar says: "One-eye, as he called him, was stealing from the rest of them (the beggars) for years. Many times he was ordered to stop, but he never did. This morning someone cut his throat." He went on to say, "I dare say, no one will ever be accused." I give the beggar another coin, and return to Reuben and our job. Soon, the way is cleared, and we pass through the gate, going on to our destination.

I feel a sense of relief, but I don't mention that to Reuben. I just give Reuben the facts and let it go at that. I don't even mention that the victim was the same man who attacked us eight years ago. We push on silently toward our job site.

Dan, coming another way, was already there. We explain our delay while we unhitch the cart, remove the plow from it, and hitch that to the team. Dan will manage the plow while Reuben guides the team. I'm to dislodge stumps and roots loosened by the plow.

Plowing begins smoothly enough, but within ten minutes, Dan collapses and falls to the ground, face down. At Reuben's quick command, the oxen halt and stand still. We drop to the ground to check Dan for any sign of life. We turn him over to his back. There is nothing: no pulse, eyes unfocused, jaw slack. Reuben's father is dead, and Reuben is instantly in shock.

I unhitch the plow from the oxen and re-hitch the cart which is nearby. Rubin and I place the body on the cart, and begin the slow laborious journey back to the stable (oxen move slowly). Finally, at the stable, I leave Reuben with the body still on the cart. Reuben unhitches the team while I go to the house to deliver the sad news to Leah.

Leah, ever in control, sends me to find a rabbi and some of her lady friends. Soon, help arrives and we move the body to the house. The women begin the preparations for burial, and the rabbi comforts the family and conducts appropriate rites.

I think we'll all sleep uneasily, or not at all, this night. The body is in the largest room in the house. Close friends are dropping in, but don't stay long. At last darkness falls, and the house becomes quiet except for the occasional muted sound of weeping. An oil lamp flickers near the body. I try to sleep, but yearn for morning. I want to put the sadness behind me. Probably we all do.

When the new day breaks, reality sets in. Friends come. Great quantities of food arrive. The rabbi is here at the home again to offer solace and comfort. The rituals occur promptly this day, the day after Dan's death. His body is buried in the plot reserved for others of his family. And now, as they say, Dan has been "gathered to his fathers."

The funeral ceremony was conducted with standard religious rites by the local rabbi, even though Dan had not followed the Pharisaic "laws" to the letter. Dan always held that his attentions to religion were rooted in a simple love of God, and a heart for the needy.

Within days, a new routine sets in. Reuben and I continue pretty much as before, but Leah becomes manager of the enterprise.

After all the years of service, Leah knows most of the usual customers, and the way Dan conducted his business.

So the work continues, month after month, and the seasons pass. Still, the business declines a bit, and that causes some concern. I wonder if Leah is finding the responsibility too stressful.

Leah and her late husband have an older son, Nathan, whom I do not know. He is three years older than Reuben. I've not heard much about him. They talk about everything else, but very little about Nathan.

As we do chores in the stable, Reuben opens up to me about his brother. Turns out that Nathan is very independent, and did not like the routine of working with his father.

Nathan, a sailor, was not present for his father's funeral because he was at sea. Nathan is a crewman on a cargo ship, calling on ports all around the Mediterranean. At roughly two-year intervals, his ship, the Jericho, calls at the port of Joppa, about thirty miles west of Jerusalem

Now, a year has passed since the death of Dan. Nathan's ship has once again docked at the Joppa port, and Nathan is here at home on leave. Because of slow and uncertain news reaching ships at sea, Dan's death is a surprise to Nathan, and his grief has the power of newness. It is sad.

With Nathan and Reuben together now, there is much reminiscing, especially at meals, and I become a listener, mostly. Nathan is obligated by contract to at least one more sea faring circuit around the Mediterranean. After that, he says he will quit the sea and come to take over the stable business as the oldest son and senior heir of his father.

That clearly pleases Leah, and does not bode particularly well for me. I suspect Nathan might consider my employment unnecessary.

I sense that my time here will end with the return of Nathan, so I privately commit to keeping an eye out for other opportunities in Jerusalem. No need to discuss this with Reuben or Leah just yet. For the time being, Leah continues to manage the business. Reuben and I continue pretty much as we have been, and Nathan goes back to sea.

One day, two Roman soldiers call on Leah to order the services of a horse-drawn wagon to move several loads of cargo from a Roman ship berthed in the Joppa port. Not only good horses and a stout wagon are required, but at least two strong men to handle the cargo.

Reuben and I fit the bill. I am now twenty-one years old, five-foot-eight, quite muscular, and blessed with good health. I have a beard, neatly trimmed, and dark wavy hair,

Anyway, Reuben and I answer the freight hauling order. We are at the Prefect Station adjacent to the Temple grounds, as instructed, to get further details. Upon studying the cargo manifest, I estimate about ten loads. The officer says that we are apparently the only hauler available. So we discuss payment and timing, and estimate ten hauling days. With the Sabbath rest, we expect eleven days for the job. Leah will have to postpone any other jobs scheduled, and help with tending the animals remaining in the stable.

The Roman pay will far exceed the pay normally earned from indigenous Judeans. If our fellow Judeans criticize us for working for the Romans, we'll simply call attention to our new motto: GOD IS OUR GUIDE.

By the third haul, the Roman agents discovered that I had a gift for languages. I could speak Hebrew fluently with either the Judean or Galilean dialect, and Aramaic (often used by the more common folk), as well.

In my now nine years in Jerusalem, I've picked up a smattering of Greek and Latin, too. So, I often fall into general conversations

50

with the Roman agents in the Prefect Station when we are off-loading cargo. One agent, in particular, likes to talk when Reuben and I take a break. His name is Marco.

Marco pulls me aside, one day, and asks if I would care to comment on the local Jewish opinion of the Roman administration of our region. My senses sharpen. Could this be some kind of trap? Does this man want to lure me into slavery? His question has dangerous implications, I think. But the man is persuasive and persistent.

Eventually, I take courage enough to tell him that there seems a strong desire among my people to govern themselves autonomously, and that there is a general resentment of Romans and Roman taxation. Otherwise, day-to-day operations seem smooth enough.

As we talk, I notice an immaculately dressed man and a beautifully gowned lady, apparently of quality, standing between two pillars on an upper balcony, looking in our direction. Marco notices my glance and asks if I know who they are. When I say "no," he tells me that the man is … Pontius Pilate. And the lady is Pilate's wife.

PILATE

While Reuben and I continue to unload this final wagon load of cargo, I try to mentally review what I've learned of the Roman rulers of our people. There are two principal rulers over this part of the Roman Empire right now. One is Pilate, and the other is Herod. They, themselves, are subject to Caesar, emperor of the vast Roman Empire.

Pilate is powerful. He is the Prefect of Judea, and a major Roman authority. He is charged with keeping peace and order in the Greater Judean District. At times he is temporarily in residence in Jerusalem (as he is now), especially when festival or religious events can swell the population to well over a hundred thousand.

Pilate's principal residence, however, is Caesarea, some seventy miles northwest of Jerusalem, and some forty miles southwest of the Sea of Galilee. Caesarea is situated on the beautiful Mediterranean coast. It is here that Rome has established a compound where major Roman administrators and military commanders and their families live while away from their native soil.

Rome dominates and controls much of the world, including all of the territories lying along the eastern shore of the Mediterranean Sea and beyond. All of this eastern area is ruled by the two agents answering to Rome: Pilate and Herod.

Pilate is a Roman. He rules all of Judea. Herod, on the other hand, is a Hebrew and a puppet of Rome. He rules the district of Galilee and lands east of the Jordan River.

Pilate is headquartered at Caesarea, on the Mediterranean coast, and Herod is headquartered at Tiberias, on the western shore of the Sea of Galilee. The two locations lie forty miles apart. Herod and Pilate are, in a sense, competitors for the favor of Rome. Their personal relationship with each other is cool but civil. Their mutual trust is weak.

The two territories ruled by Pilate and Herod have a long common border. They maintain a functional relationship to facilitate trade and travel, but the two rulers have no close friendship.

Herod, being Jewish, attends religious events in Jerusalem, even though the city itself is under Pilate's jurisdiction. At festival times, Herod and Pilate are both in Jerusalem, Herod (as a Jew), and Pilate (as the governing official).

When Pilate is in Jerusalem, he resides in the Antonia Fortress, a facility within the city, bordering the exterior of the north wall of the Temple area. It is here that he hears civil and criminal cases, and judges in the name of Rome.

Herod has a palace of his own on the west (opposite) side of Jerusalem, within the city walls. This palace is for his personal use only, because he has no official duties in Jerusalem. It serves him as a temporary residence when he visits the city. Otherwise, this palace is occupied only by limited staff and caretakers.

To be clear, Jerusalem is within Pilate's jurisdiction, not Herod's. When Herod is in Jerusalem, he is only a visitor in temporary residence.

Local control of religious laws and minor civil cases is left to the local people. The main local body of adjudication in Jerusalem is the Sanhedrin, in cooperation with the Chief Priest and the Pharisee's council, but cases that relate to the state (Rome, that is), are handled by the Prefect, ie, Pilate.

While I've been reviewing all of this in my mind, Reuben and I finish unloading the wagon, and are preparing to go backto our stable. Marco walks over and gives us our contract payment, in full, for which I sign a receipt. The job is done.

We are bidding Marco farewell when I notice Pilate striding toward us. He greets us pleasantly, thanking us for a fine job, then lingers to talk a bit.

I'm impressed by his appearance, both in clothing and demeanor. He is of average height, and may be in his late thirties, or forty. His robe is deep blue, trimmed in red. It is girded at the waist by a fine leather belt with a decorated buckle. His sandals are of the highest quality I have ever seen.

Pilate and I stand near our wagon and visit for about an hour while Reuben curries and cares for the horses, still in harness. For the most part, Reuben listens and tends the horses while Pilate and I talk. Most of the conversation consists of Pilate asking about my background, language skills, and my thoughts on the locals' opinions of the Roman administration of Judea.

Pilate may or may not be devious, but I see no problem in

discussing my people. So we talk of Jerusalem, its people and history. Pilate, in turn tells me of his life and work in Rome before being dispatched to the eastern Mediterranean for his current assignment.

Pilate and I end the day agreeably, both of us having gained something from our conversation. I think he just wanted to get an inside view of the Jerusalem people.

Pilate compliments our work once more as we climb in the wagon. Reuben and I head for the stable, and home. The horses quicken their step, and the creaks and rattles of the empty wagon speak of a successful job. We may never see Pilate again.

LEAH

Back home now, Reuben and I hand over the contract payment to Leah, and give her a verbal account of the entire job. Leah has received criticism for working for the Romans, but we think that will die down. And, the money was very good, and much needed for purchasing supplies for both the house and the stable.

Reuben is proud that Pilate praised our work, but Leah seems a little suspicious of Pilate's friendliness. Still, she did not press us. I sense that Leah's confidence in me may have weakened a little, perhaps because of my casual talks with the Romans.

This, and Nathan's plan to quit the sea in a year to take ownership of his deceased father's stable business, stimulate my thinking about leaving my friend, Reuben, and looking for a different life. The more I think about it, the more I feel the itch to move on. I will miss Reuben, and Leah too, for that matter, but I know the time has come. Sometime, before Nathan returns, I must go.

On impulse, I retrieve father's carving tools, still in my donkey pack, hanging in the stable (sadly, Millie, my donkey, died some time ago). It's been many years since I've inspected the pack. Wonder of wonders! The tools are still in good condition. Father had coated them with some type of oil (perhaps olive) and wrapped them in a soft cloth. Thankfully, I find them in very good condition.

I decide to try my hand at some simple carvings. I find some flat pieces of wood (the kind, I don't know, but it's soft) and begin to experiment. Happily, I'm soon making good progress.

I teach myself to carve, gouge, shave, smooth, depict objects, and make useful things for home use (father's specialty), especially suited to kitchen and dining service. I become adept at creating artistic scenes carved in the flat surface of these otherwise useful items; items such as plates or trays. This, I hope, avoids possible charges of creating idols that have no practical utility. I plan to offer my carvings as functional art, hoping to find appreciative buyers.

After some six months, I am brave enough to try some door-to-door sales. To my surprise, about one in ten households purchase one or more of my creations at an impressive price. I find that I can earn money this way, and that I can become an independent traveling artisan if I choose.

For several months, I continue selling in Jerusalem until I have a fairly good amount of money. Enough to travel and live in inns or guest homes if I choose, and, for the first time, really be independent. I've developed the skills and made sales, all the time keeping up my work with Reuben. And time passes quickly. Its been a year now since Reuben and I last saw Pilate.

All things considered, now is the time for me to leave Reuben and Leah, and leave the urban life of Jerusalem. Some months ago I purchased a fine mule, already trained, and fitted with an excellent saddle. I use him now on my sales routes with my carvings. He will be the perfect mount for me as I leave the city. His name is Hero.

I visit Dan's grave once more, and offer a prayer of thanksgiving to God for the open door and welcoming heart of Dan, and the way he and Leah took me in some ten or twelve years ago. They rescued me from poverty and loneliness, and set me on the road to healthy living and growing knowledge.

Exposure to the mix of people in Jerusalem helped me with language skills and a recognition of cultural variations. On top of it all, Reuben and I became lasting friends.

As I wend my way through the streets of Jerusalem, selling my art, I hear snippets of conversation that draw my attention back to Galilee, my birthplace, nearly a hundred miles north of Jerusalem.

It seems that a young man of Nazareth (in the District of Galilee) is doing very unusual things. They say he is making nature behave in strange ways. Further, he seems to have healing powers. Even more, he cites prophecies, claiming they point to this present time …. and to him.

They say he is fairly young, maybe late twenties, or early thirties. Reportedly, his parents and siblings still live in Nazareth where he grew up. He challenges and astounds wise men with his questions ... and his assertions about himself as well. They say he speaks with an aura of authority, as if he has no superior.

He is the oldest of his siblings but he no longer lives with them, they say. No one seems to know where he shelters, or where he obtains necessities. He is readily recognized in Galilee, mostly as a carpenter, they say. He is seldom seen here in Jerusalem, so far to the south. Still, there is all this talk, and I want to learn more.

I decide to return to Galilee, the place of my childhood, to see for myself. I have changed since I left the general area at the age of twelve. I am now twenty-two. I probably won't be recognized. Not only have I matured and grown a short beard, but my name is no longer the name of my youth. I'm known now only as "Caleb."

I've secretly prepared my travel pack in Leah's stable, equipping it with necessities, carving tools, and clothing. Small quantities of oats and water for Hero are included. Everything is ready. Only the announcement to Reuben and Leah remain. I do not want to do it, but I must. I can't just slip away in the night.

After a quiet breakfast, I tell Reuben and Leah that I've made a decision that will affect us all. Some seconds pass while my comment sinks in. When their attention is intensely focused, I tell them that I must leave. With raised voices, they demand to know why. Why should I give up a good home and good work, they want to know.

Laying out my rationale, beginning with the eminent return of Nathan, my desire to become independent, and the budding success of my carving skills, and sales of my work, I explain my decision.

Reuben protests loudly, Leah too, but not as vigorously as my friend Reuben. They are even more shocked when I tell them that I have gathered my few personal possessions already, and am ready to leave within the hour.

We walk to the stable together. I saddle Hero while they watch, then secure my travel pack behind the saddle. I tell them that I've packed five pounds of oats from the stable supplies, and left silver coins at the kitchen table in the house in payment. They protest the payment, but finally accept it graciously.

I lead Hero to the gate at the street and wrap his rein tips around a rail. I turn to my friends. Tears are sliding down Reuben's cheeks. His lips are quivering. He moans. Leah embraces me and whispers "God bless you, Caleb. Don't forget, you'll always be part of this family. Her eyes are dry.

Reuben and I embrace, long and hard. He is crying full-throated, like a baby. Tears fall from the cheeks of us both. I break loose, and mount Hero, reach over his neck and loosen his rein from the rail. Leaning down from the saddle, I unlatch the gate. It swings slowly open. I look at my friends, locking eyes with Reuben. He manages three words: "Why, Caleb?! Why?"

Hero responds to my touch and steps through the gate. I don't shut it. I walk Hero down the street at a steady pace. I hear Reuben sobbing. I don't look back.

Finally, I'm going to Galilee.

CHAPTER III
NEW INTEREST

REBEKAH

I'm riding out of Jerusalem on my prized mule. He is silver gray in color. And as I said before, his name is Hero.

Over time, the purchase of the mule and equipment took about a third of my earnings to date. But I still have plenty, and I expect to earn more from my carvings wherever I go.

A good mule is fast enough for me. Though not as fast as most horses, mules are more sure-footed on rough or dangerous terrain, and they are easily satisfied with rougher forage. For me, Hero is ideal. If I choose to be on foot for a while, I can board him in a public stable almost anywhere for days or weeks at a time.

Making good time, I'm more than half way to Galilee as the sun drops low. I guide Hero well off the travel path to slightly higher ground. I strip the gear from him, give him some grain and water from the carry pack, and roll out a sleeping mat. I'll tether Hero to a large shrub, and sleep in the open, under the stars. I haven't done that since I was twelve. I feel great!

For protection, I still carry father's dagger, and I've bought a sword with a two-foot blade which I carry when traveling on country travel paths. At night, in camp, Hero sounds the alarm if anyone approaches. I am in my prime and I feel reasonably safe. All seems well, and I drift off to sleep under the starry heavens.

In no time, it seems, morning sounds awaken me. Hero and I are rested and refreshed. We gear up and resume our journey. Along the way, both yesterday and today, we meet a few travel groups. We halt long enough to identify ourselves and wish all God speed.

I reach Capernaum (a city in the District of Galilee) in mid-afternoon on this second day. Stopping at an attractive inn on the coast of the Sea of Galilee, I book a room for a week. There's a public stable directly across the street, where I can board Hero.

So, I settle in to my room (the only "private" one), and wait for the evening meal here at the inn. I hope to find talkative guests at the table. Maybe I can learn something of the unusual man of my search.

While I wait, I go up to the flat roof. The view is a wonder to behold. Capernaum is situated on the northwest shore of the Sea of Galilee, and the inn overlooks the beach. I cannot see the opposite side of the sea because of the distance.

Maps show the shoreline to resemble the shape of an almond. It is larger at the north end where I am now. Here, it's maybe nine miles across. North to south, it is around thirteen miles. The Jordan River flows into it at the north, and out at the south, continuing on to the Dead Sea even farther south.

I see quite a bit of shoreline from this roof top. There are a few buildings scattered along, and many boats (apparently fishing boats), and a number of working people (probably fishermen) milling around. The scene suggests serenity.

As I descend from the roof and enter the dining area, I see two guests already seated, and another just now joining. I round out the number to four. Using the Aramaic language I say "hello." All three answer in kind, so I expect casual discussion, if any, because of the "down-home" language. We talk about the weather, traveling, occupations, the fish dinner being served, and the general area.

60

Finally, I ask if any have heard of a man in the area who is said to have some sort of extraordinary power, like a force of will. Two know nothing of this, but the third, who happens to be a fish marketer, says that there is some talk of this among some of the fishermen near the boats. He says he often overhears them discussing the young man among themselves.

Most seem to think he has some kind of power that is more than natural, but the man seems so self-assured that they don't dare to quiz him.

So that is what the guest tells me, and I am more certain than ever that I must search this man out.

The next day, I put on some old clothing, typical of a workman, perhaps down on his luck. I walk down the slope, from the inn to the shore, and begin wandering slowly among the boats and the fishermen. I don't interfere with anyone who seems preoccupied with his work.

But, soon I come across a man seated on the stern bench of his open boat, I stop and look out over the water, giving the man time to take notice of me. Then, still in Aramaic, I say: "Hello, I can't help but admire your boat." He responds genially, and we begin to chat.

I say: "My name is Caleb." He responds: "Glad to meet you. My name is Ramon. You must be new here." "I am," I say, "and I hope to be here for some time. I'm a traveling wood carver, hoping to find some customers here in Capernaum."

After some casual talk, I tell Ramon that I have heard of a young man in the area who seems to have some sort of powers, a man who virtually glows with self-confidence.

Ramon perks up and shifts his position excitedly. He knows exactly who I'm talking about. He says: "Yes, yes indeed! We just call him 'the carpenter.' None of us know much about him. He comes here often and shows a great interest in our fishing work. He's a keen observer, asks lots of questions, and is a quick learner.

"None of us quiz him much," Ramon says. "We just listen. Somehow, he seems so unusual that we just don't ask him too much. But, he is friendly. Everyone likes him."

"How old is the carpenter?" I ask. Ramon thinks about it and says: "probably in his late twenties, I would think. I believe he lives over in Nazareth, somewhere, about eight or ten miles to the southwest of here. Someone said that he is the village carpenter's son, so that's why we call him the carpenter."

"Does the carpenter work with his father?" I ask. "I think he does," Ramon says, "because sometimes he's wearing a carpenters apron over his tunic when we see him here." Ramon turns his head to look at his fishing gear, and I take that as a sign to leave, so I thank him for his time and interesting conversation, and wish him success with his fishing. He says: "Come by anytime, Caleb." So I make a mental note of his name and boat as a point of future reference, just in case.

By now, it is mid-morning. I go to the stable to get Hero and my kit of carving tools and samples of my work. I pay the stable-master, but retain my room in the inn. Mounting Hero, I ride out of the stable and head for Nazareth.

I soon reach the village which seems familiar. I was here at times as a boy. The layout of the village is familiar as Hero and I enter. I take a little time to ride through most of the streets (all dirt, of course) to locate the more prosperous looking homes. I select one, tie Hero to a post, take my samples and call on the house.

A gentleman greets me but I soon sense that he isn't interested in my art (I call it "art" now because I have become quite adept at carving figures of animals, ships, dwellings, and such on plates and trays). The gentleman is kind enough to suggest two other homes nearby where I might find some interest.

I find no interest at the next home, but at the third, I'm met by an elderly lady who, it turns out, loves to talk. Her name is Rebekah. She makes a nice appearance, stands erect, has fine features, is neatly dressed, and has lovely gray hair done up in a long braid.

She likes my art, and purchases plates depicting carved figures of two dogs. And she likes to talk. We chat … and chat … and chat some more. She invites me to sit down in her sun-room and enjoy some fresh melon from her garden. A servant boy brings the melon and we just enjoy the sweet taste and relax. Rebekah seems to like me … and she loves to talk.

Rebekah tells me much of her history, much about her family, and how Nazareth has changed since she was a girl. Her husband died four years ago, but she has a son and two daughters, all married, and living within a half-day walk. And, she has seven grandchildren that she is very proud of. Finally, I ask her if she knows the young man of Nazareth, known as the "carpenter." Her face lights up, and she warms to the subject.

"I know him," she says. "I've watched him grow from childhood. He is different, and very interesting. Let me tell you." . . .I get quiet, and listen.

CARPENTER

Rebekah settles into her cushioned chair, closes her eyes for some moments, and, finally, says:

"The man called the 'carpenter' is around thirty years old. He is away a lot, but still visits his parents on occasion. He has several brothers and sisters, all of whom have moved out now but still remain close to the family home. All have settled either in or near Nazareth. Some are married. Carpenter's parents are Joseph and Mary.

"Mary is about forty-five now. Joseph is older, maybe fifty-five. Joseph is an excellent carpenter and is well respected everywhere, especially in the synagogue. He and Mary attend every Sabbath. I know because I attend too.

"The young man, the carpenter, is often absent because he travels a lot, always walking. When he is at home, he helps his father in the carpenter shop, but even then he is often away for hours at a time, walking and talking with people, they say. I expect that someday he will not come back.

"The carpenter is a keen observer," she says. "He likes to learn. He has wide interests in nature and, especially, in people. He has a knack for linking motives to actions, and recognizing honesty and sincerity. He studies people, their values, motives, and behaviors.

"He comes to visit me sometimes and we have long, happy talks. His visits, usually every few months, started when he was much younger, little more than a boy. But for some reason his visits are becoming less frequent now. He is so wise! He talks about his childhood, and his current travels, more like wanderings.

"He told me many times that he had an exciting childhood. He usually starts with his mother's account of his birth. There was some angelic message involving his mother's pregnancy. Somehow, it fits my memory of a young pregnant Mary.

"Having lived here all my life, I remember the time when Mary became pregnant. There was gossip because Mary was not yet married to Joseph, even though they were engaged.

"Mary insists, to this day, that the pregnancy was spontaneous, and that an angel told her that God had planted the seed to create the baby within her womb. Also, that the baby would grow up and pay a great price to redeem men and women who are broken and lost. None of us dispute her, but we all wonder what this means.

"Pregnant, young and unmarried, she left for a while to visit relatives, she said. Later on, after her return, still pregnant, she told some of her friends, including me, who the relatives were that she visited. They were an older couple. I think their names were - *hmmm* - I think I recall, they were – oh yes! - Now I remember. They were Zechariah and Elizabeth.

"And, wonder of wonders, Mary found that Elizabeth was pregnant too, which was a surprise because of her age. And this you may find interesting: Zechariah is a priest!

"So Elizabeth and Mary had long happy talks about the babies in their wombs. And the two women were as amazed as anyone; one almost too old, and the other almost too young, to be expecting babies. Eventually, Mary ended her visit, and returned to Joseph here in Nazareth.

"No sooner had she left her relatives, and returned to Joseph, than a Government order was issued for a census. Because of ancestral lineage, Joseph and Mary were required to go to Bethlehem, some hundred miles to the south, to report.

"Now, with Mary nearing her term, she and Joseph set off for Bethlehem to comply with the census order. Joseph had a donkey for Mary to ride, but it was still a dangerous trip for a girl in an advanced pregnancy. Joseph, himself, walked, leading the donkey.

"A few days later, they arrived in Bethlehem, completely exhausted. They desperately needed rest, but all the inns were full. No rooms available, not even common rooms.

"Finally, a compassionate inn keeper and his wife, offered space in their stable where there would be fresh straw, but nothing else.

"There would be space outside for the donkey for which there would be feed and water. So, Joseph and Mary bedded down in a fresh bed of straw. The animals were making soft night-time sounds, a little stirring and gentle snorting." Rebekah pauses, then continues:

"In an amazing coincidence of timing, Mary began to feel signs of labor, and before the morning light, her baby was born. Joseph, himself, out of necessity, performed the services of 'midwife,' knotting the cord and cleaning the baby, a boy. Also, he was comforting Mary throughout.

"They had a clean soft towel with them in which they swaddled the new baby. Mary was tired, but, thank God, the birthing was relatively easy. This was most unusual because Mary was so young, and this was her first baby. But Mary was basically healthy and had a strong constitution, and this contributed to the successful birth and a quick recovery.

"Bethlehem is within a few miles of Jerusalem where the Temple is located. After the new little family rested a few days, they walked to the Temple in search of a priestly blessing for the infant son, and circumcision too, for it was the eighth day.

"In the Temple, they encountered a righteous man named Simeon, and a Prophetess named Anna. Both gave blessings and predictions of a great rescue of mankind. Mary and Joseph named the boy … Jesus.

"In due time, Mary and Joseph married, but not before the baby was born. The marriage was a simple affair, forgotten now by most people. But no one ever questioned their love for each other, a beautiful love."

Rebekah continued: "I think they returned to Nazareth, but when they heard that Herod The Great had ordered the killing of all male babies born in the vicinity of Bethlehem, up to two years old, they fled to Egypt, and only returned to Nazareth when the lad was about three."*

* This part of Rebekah's story is based on Matthew 1-2 and Luke 2

****

So this was Rebekah's account of the carpenter's birth. She went on to say that he was a precocious child, exhibiting amazing and mysterious wisdom, far beyond any other child his age.

Now, he is grown, and is, as she said earlier, about thirty years old. He is still seen here in Nazareth at times, usually walking with a few other men. Then, a good time passes before he is seen again.

Rebekah had worn away much of the day in conversation with me. It was so delightful. I can't thank her enough. I give her a gift of a carving of a walking man in appreciation as I bid her "shalom" and mount Hero for my return to Capernaum.

We should have about three hours before sunset, plenty of time to get back.

GALILEE

Reaching Capernaum just before dark, I leave my mule with the stable-master, and wearily cross the packed-dirt street to the inn. Climbing the stairs to my second-floor room, I lie down on my cot, and fall asleep instantly.

I must have slept soundly, twelve hours or so, before waking to the aroma of the usual breakfast provided by the inn. A good thing too. I'm just in time to take a place at the table. Two other guests, new to me, are well into their meal. We don't talk much, apparently all of us thinking of the day ahead.

After my meal of warm bread, fish chowder and figs, I return to my room, and remain there, or on the roof, for most of the day. A stairway makes the roof accessible to guests and owner alike as a place for rest and relaxation.

The roof is a great place for me to contemplate all that I had heard in Nazareth yesterday. I make notes, on parchment, of the key points from memory. Now, I give a lot of thought on what

I might do next. My art sales allow me a great deal of free time, and I hope to use that to continue my search.

I'm feeling a surge of excitement in my pursuit. I have a strong urge to spend more time at, and around, the Galilean Sea since that is where the carpenter seems to be seen most often. I decide to walk and study the entire circumference of this sea, starting tomorrow.

The day passes, and, once again, I enjoy a fine dinner. After dinner, I tell the inn-keeper my aim to learn more about the Sea of Galilee and it's people by walking the entire circumference. He is very encouraging, and even asks his wife to prepare for me a packet of food to carry with me tomorrow.

He tells me, that I'm in for a twenty or thirty mile hike, plus either fording or boating across the Jordan River twice, once at the north, where it enters the Sea of Galilee, and then at the south where it exits the Sea of Galilee and continues on for around eighty miles, entering the Dead Sea, its end-point. I know about the river already, but I do not interrupt my friend.

He thinks I won't have much trouble as long as I don't infringe on workers' (mostly fishermen) activities. "Just let them invite you to talk," he says: "because they may want to know who you are and why you are there."

"They will easily spot you as a stranger. I think you will find most of them friendly. Their dogs probably won't bother you if they don't think you are intruding on their territory. You're in for some wonderful days. If I were young and free, I would go too."

The innkeeper and I talk late, but finally I retire for the night, sleeping poorly because of excitement. I'm up before dawn, dress once again in rugged clothes, collect my packet of food, and head out on foot. Hero remains in the stable.

My starting point is just down the slope from the inn. The

heavens glow softly, promising a beautiful day. I decide to walk (meander) eastward, going along the northern breadth, then follow the shore southward to where the Sea of Galilee discharges into the Jordan River, cross the river and follow the Galilean west shoreline northward to my starting point.

As I begin my hike, I notice numerous boats in the immediate area. At a glance, I would say that about half are attended by crews preparing to launch. Maybe the others are at rest for the day, or possibly planning to launch later.

Many have sails, supported by a single mast and boom, and can likely fish the entire Galilean Sea, sometimes called a lake.

A few boats have no sail, so I suppose they depend on oars, and fish closer to shore.

I hear men calling to each other in a jumble of voices, maybe giving orders, sometimes with oaths (mild or harsh) for emphasis. Most of these fishermen are young to middle age. Some are singing, usually off-key. They are typically dressed in short tunics falling no lower than their upper thighs. I'm told that some disrobe when off-shore for freer movement.

As I walk along, I hear some names bandied about. Among the names I hear are "Simon" and "Zebedee." Then, I hear someone calling for "James."

To my delight, I see Ramon, the man I had met before. He is walking along the shore toward me. He greets me as he reaches his boat. We chat a minute. I tell him my purpose, and he gives me a few tips, things to notice like the mountains on the east and west sides and the various creeks entering the sea along the way.

At this point, Ramon cries, "Wait a minute! I think I see the carpenter way down shore. Look! Now's your chance."

I see a man in the distance, talking to some of the fishermen.

His features are clear enough, even at this distance, and I think I can recognize him if I see him again. But not today, because he is leaving, walking away, up toward the streets of Capernaum.

Ramon says nobody knows where the carpenter can be found. He just appears, unexpectedly, and then disappears again. Maybe for weeks. That being the case, I decide to watch for him over time, rather than continuing to search for him or trying to chase him down. Ramon says he will likely return someday, as suddenly as a sparrow, and then depart just as quickly.

Ramon and I talk a little more, then wish each other well (shalom), and he slides off shore using his oars as I continue my walk. I'm thinking that someday I'll meet the carpenter by chance if I keep coming to the sea where these fishermen do their work, but, for now, I want to learn about the total shore surrounding the Sea.

Several fishermen greet me, those working on shore, cleaning boats and mending nets before setting off. I think they interrupt their work to speak to me because, to them, I'm a stranger. But they are all friendly, and seem pleased when I tell them that I'm happy to be at the Sea of Galilee and am going to explore the whole shoreline.

I'm beginning to see that the people here are distinctly different from most people in the city of Jerusalem. Here, they seem simpler, in a good way. On average, I believe they are less formally educated, but they are intelligent, and are wise and knowledgeable in the ways of nature. After all, their life and work is closely tuned to the natural world.

They aren't particularly interested in philosophical arguments or discussions. They "read" the weather signs, by which they "know" when and where the fishing is good, and they understand and prepare for the seasons.

They speak Hebrew with a regional accent or dialect. It is understandable, but unlike that of the more urbanized people of Jerusalem, who mistakenly consider the Galilean version humorous, or a mark of inferiority.

Alternatively, and locally, these Galileans often speak Aramaic (a declining language), liberally seasoned with colloquialisms common to the region. I can easily communicate in Aramaic because I remember much of it from my youth (my now secret first twelve years in this region).

These people respect their rabbis, and attend synagogue and tend to accept the rituals without question. Their religious basics remind me of Dan of Jerusalem (my deceased benefactor) whose relationship with the Almighty, he said, was based on "simply loving God and caring for the needy." Some of these fishermen "talk" to God throughout the day - about fishing, weather, family, safety; things like that.

I continue my walk. There are few obstacles. Sometimes a fallen tree, or driftwood. Once, I came across a few cottages, and an abandoned boat with serious hull damage, left long ago to rot. Ten hours pass before I reach the southern shore of the sea, where a measure of it flows through a natural channel to continue its life as the Jordan River.

Once I cross the river, I will still have ten or fifteen hours of walking, and ten or twelve miles of shoreline to travel up the west side before reaching my starting point. I'll have to sleep in the open tonight. It will be dark in two hours, so I must be on the lookout for a suitable spot.

Suddenly, I get a whiff of wood smoke. My senses come alive. I've seen no one for at least two hours, so what can this be? I squint my eyes and stand still, and listen. Voices float faintly to my ears, but I cannot make out words. Then, a laugh. Sounds like a woman's laugh. Maybe it's a family. I proceed cautiously.

Soon, they spot me. The voices stop. They are gathered around a fire. I advance slowly, hearing nothing but the crackle of the fire. I raise both arms to indicate no harm. Several men stand. Others remain seated. One man walks toward me. I halt and wait for the man to reach me. We finally meet some fifty yards short of the group.

We greet cautiously. I say: "I'm alone, walking the shoreline all around the sea. I think I'll be walking at least fifteen hours more. My name is Caleb." The man says: "Shalom, my name is Josh. It'll soon be dark. Where will you stop for the night?" I say: "I'll have to sleep on the beach."

Josh remains silent for a long pause, thinking. I'm silent too. We are holding eye contact. At last, Josh invites me to meet his group. He tells them who I am and why I'm here. They want to know why I'm walking.

I tell them that I'm new in Capernaum, am excited about the area, and just want to become familiar with the shoreline – which I consider beautiful. They seem to like this. There are men, women, and older children in the group, maybe twenty or so. They seem prepared to camp where they are, at least for the night.

A pot of stew is suspended over the fire. One of the men, apparently the spokesman, invites me to eat with them, and to bed down near them. He says it would be safer than being alone. I agree, thinking that I might learn who they are and what they are doing.

As the group begins to relax, and the stew warms our tummies, I sense some sort of excitement and eager anticipation among them. Chatter and laughter returns, especially among the women and children. From the talk among them, I can tell that they are traveling on foot, probably for some distance, it seems, because of the gear they have. Maybe they are on some sort of pilgrimage.

Some of the men and I begin some small talk. I do my best to display friendliness. Soon, we're talking about our work and our families, and our hopes. Turns out, the group formed up north, some forty miles north of the Galilee Sea. Their destination is somewhere down the Jordan River where they've heard from others that a spellbinding, fiery, speaker (maybe a prophet, even) is drawing large crowds.

It is said that this engaging speaker has a way of causing people to see evil in their lives, which, needs to be rejected, and that they should strive for pureness in their lives. Many are convicted in conscience, they say, and their new lives are endorsed and revived by a ritual in the river called baptism.

This does not sound like the carpenter, the man of my search. But what these people tell me is very interesting. I begin to think of this man as "the man of the Jordan."

I think I'll complete my hike around the shore of the Sea of Galilee tomorrow, and if I have not seen the carpenter by then, I may go on my own, riding Hero, to investigate the man of the Jordan. I'll probably find the carpenter later.

I move some distance away from this friendly group and bed down for the night … alone.

I don't know about the man of the Jordan, except what I've learned from these travelers. He seems to be a new phenomenon, maybe a "flash," here today and gone tomorrow.

But, if he is impacting men by the hundreds, or thousands, I want to know who he is before he somehow disappears. Is he making a mark on history? I must find out! I want to finish my walk without delay. Then, I'll retrieve Hero and go down the Jordan.

After a night under the stars, I gather my gear and resume my walk. Along the way I note the things I see; a few boats and fishermen, mostly, and some existing footpaths, leading inland from the shore, probably used by humans for centuries.

Boats appear in greater numbers as I get closer to Capernaum, the end of my circuit. More fishermen too. The sun sets while I'm still walking, but, fortunately, a three-quarter moon lights my way back to the inn. Once again, I enter the inn, climb to the second floor and the comfort of my room. I sleep solidly until the morning sounds awaken me.

At mid-morning, I find the innkeeper sweeping floors and cleaning up. He stops his labor to greet me and chat. He happily listens to my tale of experiences, and when I tell him of the travelers, he questions me closely, for he, too, has heard of the man of the Jordan.

Talk of him has been around for months, he says. Guests who have encountered the man in their travels can't stop talking about him. Their lives seem to have acquired a new purpose, a new spark of energy and enthusiasm. It's puzzling but true. Guests tell him, he says, that the man can be found some eighty miles, or so, south of Capernaum, on the east side of the Jordan River.

I tell the innkeeper that I'm going to find the "man of the Jordan," but first I'll spend some time at the inn to carve, sell door to door, and restore my purse.

I carve and sell, carve and sell. For two weeks, I carve and sell. My best customers are among the wealthiest, often wives or widows. I meet many, and restore my funds. Now, I'm ready to go.

My new focus is the man of the Jordan.

CHAPTER IV
DIVERSION

SEARCH

Early one morning, I bid the innkeeper "shalom" and thank him and his wife for their hospitality. I clear out of my room and cross the dirt street to the stable. Hero, my mule, is clean and rested, and ready for travel.

I visit with the stable-master for a bit, clear any open charges, and turn my attention to Hero. I saddle him, and place my dual leather carry bags snugly behind the saddle. I pack my gear in the bags, and strap my sword to my belt. I have enough grain and water for Hero, and enough food for myself (this, in case we don't find an inn on the way). We set off. The sun has risen an hour ago. The weather is favorable.

Instead of picking our way along the river bank, we take the travel path, directly south through Samaria, going all the way to a village near Old Jericho (two-day trip). This will put me within a couple of miles of my target area on the lower Jordan River, in the vicinity of reported sightings of the "man."

Downriver, from the reported sightings, the Jordan flows into the Dead Sea. To the west, some fifteen or twenty miles, is the city of Jerusalem where I grew from a boy of twelve to manhood; the Temple and top religious leaders are located there too, including the Chief Priest, Caiaphas.

Surrounding Jerusalem are numerous villages, occupied mostly by laborers, shepherds, and others, some out of work.

Maybe I'll find out more about the "man" from the locals there. Anyway, I'm just anticipating.

Riding along, all sorts of thoughts drift through my mind throughout the day. Could the man of the Jordan really be a prophet? What is the attraction? They say he lives a rough life in the wild.

Hero is demonstrating his stamina today, keeping a steady pace, hour after hour. But now we're nearing our half-way point on this trip. I'm looking for suitable ground, off the travel path, where Hero and I can sleep once more under the stars. We're coming to a likely spot now. We leave the travel path and make camp. We'll sleep this night under the twinkling cover of distant stars. And I'll dream of God himself singing a peaceful lullaby for us, declaring his eternal love and care.

At sun-up, I curry Hero a bit, and we both eat (oats for him and dried fruit for me). We share some water from the travel pack. I saddle up and we resume our travel south.

Hero carries me steadily, without complaint. At noon we stop for a short rest and a bite. I give him some water. Then, we're back on the travel path. It is mid-afternoon when we see a turn-off toward Old Jericho. We take that trail until we find a small village with a very modest inn, more like a home. It's rather small but, at least, there is an available stall for Hero. Everything looks clean and neat.

The owners come out to greet me. They seem very glad at the prospect of a guest. I doubt if they have many because their home is well off the main north-south travel path. It is, however, on a minor east-west travel path running from Jerusalem to the Jordan River, and beyond after fording it.

The river is suitable for fording at this point, they say, and the path continues on eastward on the other side. By chance, it seems, I have chosen a home (hardly an inn) that is ideally located for my purpose.

76

The owners are determined to treat me as family. I tell them my name is Caleb, and they give me their informal names: Zeb and Leah, I think to myself that "Zeb" may be short for Zebulon or Zebedee, and Leah may be his wife's given name; the name "Leah" reminds me of Reuben's mother in Jerusalem.

Zeb and Leah take me under their wings, and do everything they can to see to my comfort. I tell them I may be here for several days, and I pay in advance for seven. They allocate the entire second floor for my private use. It is very small, but cozy. Zeb will take care of Hero.

Leah proves to be an excellent cook. Supper is roast chicken and a mixture of root vegetables, plus fresh bread and new honey. I'm careful not to overeat, but it's so tempting. When I tell them of my quest, they become vibrant with enthusiasm.

Turns out, they have seen the man at the river. They tell me that they stand on the fringes of the crowd, and watch and listen. Crowds usually gather a bit before mid-morning. They come on foot, mostly, walking along the travel-path fronting the couple's home.

Zeb says: "You'll see them tomorrow morning, walking along, sometimes in clusters, full of talk, and hope, too. Sometimes I talk with a few on their return. Some say they come again and again, proud, even, of the number of times."

My hosts tell me that the river-man's name is John. He comes from northern Judea somewhere, from a priestly family. Zeb thinks for a moment, and says: "If I remember right, John's father's name is Zechariah. And his mother's name is Elizabeth. They say Zechariah is a priest, very old now." John is a spellbinder. They say his voice carries well, and is amplified by the gentle water surface and the river banks.

I tell my hosts that I mean to go to the site tomorrow. Leah promises that I won't be sorry, and that she will put together a little lunch for me to carry. Finally, we all go to our beds, but

I find it hard to sleep. Can't stop thinking about tomorrow. Something keeps tugging at my memory, and it nags me. Finally, I remember!

THOSE NAMES! I DO REMEMBER!! Those were the names, maybe of the very same people, the relatives, visited by the young pregnant Mary, on the occasion related to me by Rebekah, the lady in Nazareth that I visited a few weeks ago.

Then it dawns on me! John of the Jordan and the carpenter of Nazareth are related; must be, in some degree, but I may never know exactly what it is. My mind is spinning: "Will I ever get to sleep?"

I must have drifted off at last, for my next conscious sensation is the wonderful aroma of breakfast.

Leaving Hero in the stable, I start my two or three mile walk to the Jordan soon after breakfast, glad for the lunch Leah packed for me. I meld in with other walkers, but I don't get into conversations. I feel as wide-eyed as a new-born baby, expecting to see and hear things I've never seen before.

The walkers are not crowding each other, but when looking ahead and behind, I see nothing but walkers moving in a steady stream. They are energized and loud in conversation. I move along, keeping pace. The river is still some distance ahead, but, as we come closer, I notice the boisterous behavior begins to subside, and the voices become softer.

I, along with the rest, slow down. We fan out as we come nearer to a widely spread group of people who are already there, standing still. They are mostly silent, only a little murmuring here and there. If one could look on the crowd from a tree-top, he would see that the crowd had voluntarily formed in such a way that everyone could look toward a specific point in the river.

I join the group at the outer fringe where I can see not only the crowd, but the place of interest as well. I see a hut, of a temporary nature on the far side of the river. Three young men stand near the hut. Someone whispers to me that they are John's students, or disciples.

We wait. The crowd is hushed.

JOHN

We continue to stand quietly. Looking over my shoulder, I note that the stream of walkers has diminished to almost none. It seems that people, in general, know when they should be here.

My near-by neighbor whispers that John's disciples roam Jerusalem and the villages, inviting everyone to hear their teacher on certain days, and to be in place by mid-morning so as not to miss the opening.

I sense a stirring in the crowd! I look intently toward the hut across the river. The river is fordable. Even so, the water will reach knee-high in several places.

The crowd emits a noticeable gasp when a man steps out of the hut. My senses are on high alert. My eyes are focused on the man. It's John! A man of about thirty, dressed as a man of the wild, wearing a camels-hair garment, covering his torso and upper thighs. The garment is made so that part of it is draped over his left shoulder. His right shoulder is bare. His arms are bare. He wears sandals with sturdy soles and strong laces winding nearly to the knees.

Facial hair is plentiful. It looks ruffled, as if wind-blown, and it is brown, or a rich tan. His skin looks tanned, probably due to long exposure to the sun. He is of average height, well-built and muscular. He is making his way across the river, accompanied by two disciples. The other disciple remains at the hut.

They say he lives on locusts and wild honey. I would guess the locusts are roasted. There must be other food, but no one I whisper with seems to know. He does leave the river at times, they say, to walk through the streets of Jerusalem, and he keenly notes the behaviors and the talk of the people, especially those of the religious and ruling set. These, in turn, are aware of John, and frequently ask their subordinates what they have learned about the man.

Now, John and his disciples are nearly across the river. John comes to a rock ledge on the near-side. The ledge extends from the shore into the river a short way, a natural platform, or stage. The ledge is fairly flat on top, and the top stands a little above the river surface.

The ground that I and the crowd stand on rises gently from the river, giving most of us a clear view of John and those nearest to him. No one approaches him by more than ten feet. My neighbor whispers that later John will invite us to come to him, one by one.

When John reaches the ledge, he steps up to its surface, dismisses his disciples, and faces the crowd. The two disciples sit down on the shore, near to John.

John stretches both arms wide and slightly raised, the palms of his hands open toward the crowd. Then he speaks distinctly and loudly in a clear, commanding voice, a voice amplified somewhat by the water and the lay of the land. He shouts loudly:

"BLESSINGS FROM THE GOD OF OUR FATHERS!!
(pause - relaxes his arms - and continues)

WHETHER YOU KNOW IT OR NOT - YOU'VE COME TO HEAR ME TELL YOU WHAT SORRY PEOPLE YOU ARE IN THE SIGHT OF GOD. BUT FIRST - I WANT YOU TO KNOW THAT GOD LOVES YOU.

(and he continues until mid-day)

He reminds us, with force, of the ways we displease God. Some of the things he hammers on today are: stealing, envy, cheating, adultery, hate, drunkenness, vile language, dishonesty, deceit, . . . and much much more. He calls them "sins," and he calls all of us standing before him "sinners."

He speaks plainly, using the common, vernacular-spiced, language, easily understood by everyone, even those with the most basic of vocabularies.

He moves immediately into his subject: the evil thoughts and deeds that plague humanity. One after another, he delves into them. He directs everyone to look inwardly to discover abominations within themselves. His gestures add perfect emphasis.

He directs each to look at his own sorry life. To my surprise, his listeners do not seem offended. The crowd is quiet, except for some who are sobbing, or maybe groaning.

John seems blessed with a natural attraction. People are drawn to him, even when he is admonishing them in the strongest of terms. He keeps urging everyone to look within themselves, to look for the destructive evil within them, each of us. He speaks to the crowd, but it seems to each individual that the words apply directly to them. I begin to feel it myself. But I am determined to remain an observer.

John even condemns some of the religious leaders, especially those of the Pharisee sect.

Not only that, he levels his fire on the national rulers, even on Herod, because Herod took his brother's wife as his own (this is Herod Antipas, son of Herod the Great).

I think these accusations will someday come back to haunt him, but John is brave in his indictments. I'm sure the word will get back to these proud rulers from their subordinates; some undoubtedly scattered among the crowd as spies this very day.

The man beside me befriends me when he learns that this is my first time here. He tells me that one day, recently, several Pharisee leaders, clad in their rich distinctive robes, with tassels and all, came to see for themselves just who this John is.

John called them to the front, near him, and declared their evil nature to them and to the astonished crowd. He loudly proclaimed them to be hypocrites, serpents, vile people, haughty, and speaking words that seem as useless as dark echoes from the grave.

My new friend continued, saying that the Pharisee's tried to counter the charges, but were ineffective, and were humiliated when the crowd began to laugh. They slunk away, probably wishing they had not come, and they were sure to carry a distorted version of this encounter back to their colleagues and superiors.

I can see that John is bypassing the man-made religious rules that have grown like clinging weeds over the ages. He brings the common people into closer and more direct contact with God than their top religious leaders ever do. I see that John is brave and unafraid. But I wonder if this will, someday, be his doom.

Finally, at John's invitation, many of those in the crowd advance to enter the water of the Jordan. One of the two disciples helps each penitent person, one by one, into the water, to be symbolically cleansed by the baptism of John. They are first submerged, then raised upright again.

That done, the second disciple helps the penitent out of the river. Sometimes, I'm told, the baptisms continue until mid-afternoon, or later.

Then, as excitement abates, I turn back toward the inn. I remember my lunch, and enjoy it on the way.

Zeb and Leah are eager to hear all about my day. They had

both been to one of John's meetings, so we began making comparisons of our experiences. There were a lot of similarities, but the various evils spoken of were not all the same, though many were. Obviously, John varies the message somewhat, and that encourages people to make repeat visits.

Zeb has heard of the incident with the Pharisees, so that was no surprise. This leads us to discuss the rules and rituals that the priesthood requires of its people, especially the requirements for donations or purchases of sacrificial objects, such as doves or lambs.

We wonder how all of these rules started. There must have been a first rule, then others added, one by one, until now an entire class of priests and their assistants are needed to see that they are imposed.

We talk by the light of an oil lamp late into the night. Finally, Leah douses the lamp and we take to our beds. I use the next morning to record my experiences on parchment, and, after a mid-day meal, I saddle Hero for a ride into nearby Jerusalem just for a break.

I ride by the stable to see Reuben and his mother, Leah. Both welcome me with great joy. They assure me that they are doing very well. They expect Nathan back from the sea very soon, and still expect him to take over the stable business, as he is his father's heir.

Leah has heard of John. There seems to be considerable talk of him in Jerusalem, mostly in the form of conjecture as to who he is. Some think he is a prophet, maybe Elijah, reincarnated. Others consider him a powerful preacher, or just an engaging curiosity.

Finally, I bid my friends shalom for the day. Mounting Hero, he and I continue through the streets of Jerusalem, going past the gate favored by beggars. They are still there. But not Ike, of course. You may remember, he was killed by the beggars. No one was charged or convicted, so I hear. I ride slowly throughout the city to reminisce, not calling on anyone in particular. Not yet, anyway.

Late in the day, I return to the inn, and the warmth of Zeb and Leah. It is coincidence that Leah's name is the same as Reuben's mother's. Leah of the inn is an even better cook than Reuben's mother.

I decide to make two or three more visits to John at the river, so I pay Zeb in advance for an extra week at the inn to give me plenty of time.

Except for the stirring admonitions of John at the Jordan, life here is serene. Zeb and Leah treat me like part of the family, and I am at ease. They take delight in telling me of their six grown children, now with homes of their own, and many grandchildren. Zeb, Leah, and I, genuinely enjoy each other.

John has become the talk of the entire region of Judea, and well beyond. And, he is controversial. He has criticized powerful people. He has raised concerns and suspicions among the highest religious leaders and the rulers of the land; they, in turn, are sharply critical and suspicious of him. But John's followers remain steadfastly devoted to him, and are highly supportive.

As I continue to go to John's meetings, I notice that he often references prophesies by Isaiah of a future leader with a great purpose. And I notice another thing, something intriguing. Something said so often that the utterance has become expected.

He repeatedly declares, day after day, that: **"One greater than I is to come, one of whom I am unworthy even to loosen his sandals." ***

* **See Mark 1:7**

GREATER

Once more, I ease into the flow of walkers going to the river; this is my eighth time. I feel a need to go this one more time before heading back to Galilee to resume my search for the carpenter. But one more time with this gathering won't much affect my plans.

As we walk along the travel path to the Jordan, hundreds of us, the group chatter has a different feel than it did when I first walked with them nearly three weeks ago. There is less talk of John, and more of the mystery man.

Oh, sure, John is still a big part of the talk, but the general mix has changed. Now, for one thing, many people are questioning who John really is; and, for another, just who is the mystery man that is yet to come.

Some are saying that John **must be** a former prophet, come back in the flesh. He seems too special to be an ordinary man.

We are still walking, but the pace is slowing as the river comes into view. Talk of the mystery man grows stronger as our pedestrian line spreads out into the crowd of early arrivals. Will this be the day?! How will we know?!

The group today is the largest that I've seen. The weather is favorable. The birds are chirping. Raptors soar high overhead. Tree-dwelling creatures rustle the leaves. And it promises to be a beautiful day.

As we meld into the standing group ahead, I notice, as usual, a quietness. The boisterous talk on the walk has ceased. I hear the whispering of near neighbors. Other than that, nothing but a few coughs and sneezes, and maybe some shifting feet. The entire crowd is a picture of patience.

Across the river, the hut and the three disciples are in place. The disciples are assessing the crowd, always alert to any hint of trouble, to any potential disturbance, or anything at all out of the ordinary.

I'm amazed that John has not been taken by either the Roman or the ecclesiastical authorities for questioning, or imprisonment. It's no wonder that the two disciples are on alert. His assertions of hypocrisy and evil often fly in the face of the establishment, both the religious and the ruling class.

From my vantage point on the outer fringe of the group, I can scan most of the crowd. I look slowly from right to left, and then back to the right. There's nothing unusual, no one in uniform, especially no one in Roman military uniform.

At mid-morning, John emerges from the hut, and fords the river with two disciples as he always does. He blesses the crowd and begins his oration from the rock ledge that serves as his stage.

His speech always mesmerizes me. It's his voice, so clear and far-reaching, and his gestures and overall body language, and his countenance (always changing). In short, John speaks not only with his voice, but with his whole body, his whole being. I am not conscious of time, only of John.

John has been speaking, forcefully and vigorously, for about an hour. But he suddenly stops. He stands as still as a statue, his stance and gesture of the previous moment frozen in place. He seems to be staring past the crowd. Silence hangs in the air. Finally, his body loosens.

He is standing erect again, facing the crowd. He turns his body a quarter turn, like an archer's stance, extends his left arm, and points to the back of the crowd, in the direction of the travel path. In the clearest voice I've ever heard, John shouts: **"Behold – the lamb of God."** * The crowd pivots as a single body, and looks to the rear. I do too. John's words will be etched in my brain, I think, forever.
*** See John 1:29**

Immediately, upon hearing the word ... "lamb," I think of "sacrifice." And I ask myself: "Will there be a sacrifice today?" Is "lamb" symbolic of this man? What is going to happen? Except for the sound of shifting feet, all is quiet ... that is, until John speaks again.

John continues to look over and beyond the crowd, faces the man at the rear, extends both arms toward him, and says: "Come."

The man advances slowly, but at a steady pace. A pathway through the crowd opens as though by plan (but there is no plan). I am standing at the edge of the now open pathway, watching. The pace of the man continues. As he nears my location, I'm struck by a feeling of recognition.

The average height and build of the body, the complexion, the hair (dark and ruffled, like John's), the calmness and sense of purpose; these features are all there, and, somehow, seem familiar. Then it dawns on me. THIS IS THE CARPENTER!!

This is the man of Nazareth, of Galilee, the man I saw talking with the fishermen on the shore of the Sea of Galilee. The man considered to be unique by those who know him, to have powers unlike other men. Yes, I have no doubt, this is the Carpenter!! The carpenter is wearing a cream-colored robe. Only his head, his lower arms and sandal clad feet are exposed. He and John don't seem to be strangers. Yet, there is an aura of formality between them. There is not a sound from the crowd. We all watch and listen.

The carpenter says in a clear voice: **"John, I've come to be baptized."** * John loudly objects. A disagreement {not an argument) follows. John says, emphatically: "No, you should baptize me! It wouldn't be right for me to baptize you. You are holy!"

But the issue comes to rest when John finally agrees to baptize

*** See Matthew 3:14**

the man I know as the carpenter. John asks: "What name should I use when I baptize you?" The man said: "Jesus."

So, with John's disciples assisting, one holding the carpenter's robe, John baptizes Jesus in the Jordan River.

It seems that a great voice speaks, or is it distant thunder?

John's disciple assists Jesus as he comes out of the water. The disciple returns the robe, and receives a "thank you."

Silence has returned, both at the water's edge and in the crowd. In a short time, the silence gives way, slowly but steadily, until the prevailing sound becomes a murmur. While people are talking, Jesus quietly walks along the river bank, upstream, around a bend, and out of sight.

John regains the attention of the crowd, quiets us, and declares that we have just witnessed a holy happening, and it will not be proper for us to proceed in our usual way today. Therefore, today's meeting is concluded. Our next meeting will be in two days. John blesses us all, and seals the day with "Amen." We begin to disperse.

Dazed, I return to the inn. It is almost impossible to describe the day to Zeb and Leah, but I try. Finally, I give up. They see that I need to be alone. Leah brings me food and drink, and assures me that she and Zeb will be around if I need them. I love them.

I take my carving set and wood pieces to the back garden, and spend the rest of the day carving. I have been carving in my spare time all along, and have built up my stock. Tomorrow, I'll go to Jerusalem one more time, hoping to make some sales to replenish my purse.

My engravings on the surfaces of various plates and trays continue to improve. And I find that buyers are willing to pay more, and buy more, than ever before.

Zeb, Leah, and I, have a late supper and an early bed. I feel spent. But I must have slept well because as morning breaks, I awaken feeling refreshed. We have pleasant conversation at breakfast, all three of us talking about our plans for the day.

I tell them that I will spend the day in Jerusalem, selling carvings, and will return to the inn in the evening. I find it hard to tell them that I will leave for Capernaum tomorrow.

But I do tell them, so as not to surprise them at the last minute. Zeb and Leah express regret, but they understand. So, with a full tummy, I mount Hero, and set off with my carvings.

I see that Hero is glad for the exercise of the trip. I go directly to the wealthier area of Jerusalem, and start calling on likely-looking homes. As the morning progresses, I find that, on average, about every third home owner purchases one or more of my carvings.

At mid-day, I happen across a dealer in gold. My eyes fall on a beautiful slender chain. I inspect it, and find it to be a perfect fit for the small wooden star that Ruthie, my little sister, gave to me when we were children.

You may remember that my mother and father, and eight year old Ruthie, were kidnapped by bandits on a travel path some twelve years ago. I was twelve at the time nearly thirteen. At father's frantic urging, during the melee, I managed to escape with our donkey. That is when I changed my name to Caleb.

I pray that my family is still alive. I keep Ruthie's gift suspended from my neck at all times. She was so proud to be able to give it to me. She "made" it herself from a wood scrap left from our father's carvings. She may have been six or seven at the time. Her star is just wood, but it is my most treasured possession.

I purchase the gold strand and string it through the star to replace the frayed cord that has held it all these years. I feel good. Thoughts of my family always lift my spirits.

I resume selling, and my carvings are gone by mid-afternoon. Word is out that Herod is in his Jerusalem palace for a few days (normally, he is in Tiberius, on the western shore of the Sea of Galilee). I steer clear of the palace, and the presence of soldiers, because reports are that the soldiers are questioning everyone about John.

Late in the day, Hero and I return to the inn … for the last time.

BANDITS

Breakfast is extraordinary this morning, my last morning with Zeb and Leah. The atmosphere (the aura) around the breakfast table is warm and comforting, as if marking something very special.

It's so touching when I realize that Zeb and Leah are showing their warmest feelings for me. We linger over stews, porridge, fruit and bread, and review our time together. We promise to try to meet again, but we know that probably won't happen.

It is a poignant moment when we walk to the little stable together, and I begin saddling Hero, and strap my sword to my belt. We hug. I feel Leah's tears. She puts something in my hand. Lunch. She has made me one more of her wonderful lunches: most likely meat, cheese, bread, and dried fruit.

I mount Hero, reach down to touch their hands once more, and let Hero know that it's time. We head west at a slow walk. I do not look back. When we pass the first bend in the travel path, beyond sight of Zeb and Leah, I nudge Hero into a faster pace. In a short time, we reach the intersecting path leading north to Galilee.

The sky is overcast today, fitting to my mood upon leaving my friends. Soon, I overtake and pass two travel groups, on foot, and somewhat apart, also going north. We greet and wish each other safe travel, but I do not linger with either group.

Eventually, I see a small village ahead. It's mid-morning, so I stop to give Hero a short rest and a drink. A few village idlers are hanging about. They like to visit with travelers, and maybe sell something, usually food or drink. And, they gossip.

There are reports, they say, of bandits to the north, the direction of my travel. I linger, trying to decide whether to look for an inn, or to go on. Upon finding that the last report is two days old, I decide to continue on my way. Hopefully, the bandits have moved on.

Hero settles to a steady walk. He is young and does not tire quickly. The rhythmic motion of the saddle is comforting to me. I eat figs from Leah's lunch package while riding. Hero seems content, so we keep going. We seem to have the travel path to ourselves, for now.

The cloudiness gives way to a warming sun which feels good, but creates a glare that hampers long range visibility. My tunic's hood would shade my eyes, but it would also reduce my side vision and my hearing, so I leave it at my back. Being alone, I try to be vigilant. One can never be too cautious on the lonely portions of the travel path.

Uh-oh. Up ahead I see something moving. I rein Hero in so I can look more carefully. The object seems to be a single person, on foot. I study the surroundings around both me and the other person. I estimate the distance between us to be a half mile, so I can't make out details of the person; man or woman, old or young, armed or not, I cannot tell.

I wonder why this person is in this remote place alone. My senses sharpen. I stand in the stirrups and wait, one hand shading my eyes. The object seems to be moving slowly, or maybe standing still.

Some boulders and scrubby pines are on the left at the place of concern. On the right, the ground is very rough and covered with loose stones, some as large as melons. I sit in the saddle, and move Hero along, slowly, keeping an eye on the person and the surroundings.

The image grows as I progress, and I can now make out that he is a man, mature but not old. I get closer and closer, and finally I'm along side. The man halts me by grabbing Hero's halter, and telling me that he is hungry.

At this, two other men quickly emerge from the scrubby trees on the left, holding raised daggers, one near Hero's throat. One man orders me to dismount, but I have already loosed the scabbard flap and grasped my sword. The sword slips out of the scabbard as slick as a melon seed, and I swing it over Hero's head and down on the arm of the man holding Hero's halter.

Things are happening with the speed of lightning. I glimpse a spurt of blood as I take a backhand swing of my sword toward the man on the other side, the man holding the dagger near Hero's throat. He jumps back, and so does the third man. They stand as if in shock. Hero is prancing vigorously, but still in my control.

The man I struck is sitting on the ground, looking at his right arm. The hand has been severed above the wrist, and blood is gushing in strong spurts. He will be dead in five minutes for sure.

I glimpse horses under the trees, and suspect these bandits may have accomplices, or, if not, may themselves mount the horses and chase me down. At this point, I know that I must escape, or fight against long odds.

I turn Hero off the travel path onto the rough rocky ground, give him a kick of my heels, and he begins picking his way through the loose rocks. Horses aren't as sure-footed on loose rocks, so I think that even with deliberate pacing, my mule will clearly outdistance the horses.

A few minutes later I turn in the saddle and scan the area

toward the attack point. I see no pursuers. The bandits have not followed.

The sun is sliding below the horizon now. It will soon be dark. A thin crescent moon has risen but it will give too little light for further travel. I must search for a bit of higher ground for a dry camp. I don't see or hear any sign of danger now. We come to a slight hill suitable for waiting out the night. I tether Hero to a nearby shrub, give him some water from my supply, and a pint of oats.

Gathering suitable rocks to create a backrest for myself, I sit down to rest. I will try to stay awake through the night, on guard. Tomorrow will be a new day.

MISSING

Most of the night, I watch the stars. They seem to move as one across the night sky, none losing its place among the others. The night sky is one of the most beautiful sights I've ever seen.

I don't know how, but I did stay awake all night. We were not attacked, which is a relief, but I am weary and probably not as alert as I should be. Anyway, the early morning light has stirred Hero. I tend to him, saddle him, and load my gear.

I decide to let Hero pick his way north for a few miles before going back to the travel path. It is slow going, but we finally return to the main path.

I see no one in any direction, so we resume our northward travel. Still, I keep a sharp eye in all directions. Around mid-morning, I see a village and a small inn. I'm so exhausted from a sleepless night that I can hardly stay in the saddle.

So I turn in, book a cot and a stall, and settle in for a day and a night, to rest. The innkeeper had not heard of any recent bandit activity, so he says. This may be the truth …. or he may be an accomplice to the bandits, and providing protection for them.

When I tell him of my experience, he becomes very concerned for several reasons. First, he shows concern for my well being, my health, my belongings, and my mule. I assure him that I am all right, only shaken and exhausted.

Then he questions me sharply, wanting to know just where the attack occurred, how many attackers, and whether I have any idea where they may be going, south or north. Fear of bandits is not only bad for business, he says, but bandits are also a danger to the inn itself. I'm still not sure I trust this innkeeper, even if his concern sounds real.

Bandits have been known to take over an inn, robbing goods and money, and disappearing. So, of course, he is concerned if he is truthful. And, as we talk, he apparently concludes that my account is probably true (he is cautious). He thanks me for the alert, and promises to warn folks as they come by.

He further said that he will keep the noise of business as quiet as he can through this day so that I can get my needed rest. And, not to worry, he would see to my mule. Not all rooms have doors, but mine does. I bar it with heavy furniture, just in case.

I must have slept through the rest of the day, and then the night, for my next conscious sense was of morning sounds, and the aroma of food. Upon rising, cleaning up, and having breakfast, I have some pleasant talk with the innkeeper and a woman that he says cooks and cleans for him. I bid all shalom, and go to the stable.

Hero had been fed and watered, so I saddle him and place my goods behind the saddle and head out. A misty rain is floating in the air, but it soon gives way to broken clouds and sun. I feel great! And rested! My mistrust of the innkeeper seems in error.

Today's trip is calm and routine. I eat the rest of Leah's lunch, and give some oats and water to Hero, and we travel on. Finally, in the late afternoon, I see Capernaum in the distance. I wonder if the only private room at the inn is still available. It's more expensive, so it is often available. I ride in to the stable where Hero boarded on my first visit, and make arrangements for an extended stay.

Thankfully, I find that my favorite room at the inn across the hard dirt street is still available. I check in with Tobias, the innkeeper, who is as congenial as ever. Tobias is older than I am by at least a generation. We came to enjoy long conversations together when I was here previously. This time we talk for hours.

Tobias is fascinated by my recent experiences. We break it up when other guests arrive, straight off a journey, and Tobias turns to tend to them.

I pay to reserve my room for a month. This depletes my funds, so I must get busy with my carvings, and try to make some sales.

After the evening meal at the inn's dinner table, I arrange my things in my rented room and turn in for a good night's sleep in a comfortable setting.

A new day comes, and I settle down to work. I take four days too carve some of my more popular items, then make sales calls for two days. This is successful, so now my purse is somewhat re-funded.

At last, I'm free to visit the waterfront, renew contacts, and ask about the carpenter. I have been away for five weeks.

I walk down the slope from the inn to the shore. It is just now day-break, a likely time to find some fishermen before they set out. I pass a few crews that seem too busy to visit, but then I see Ramon sauntering along toward me and his boat, seemingly in no hurry. We soon make eye contact. He smiles broadly. So do I.

We greet with a hug, as though we had been friends forever. I offer to help him with launching, but he would rather find out where I have been. We sit on the port gunnel of his boat for a long time while I relate my experiences, including the surprise appearance of the carpenter. This interests Ramon to no end.

We speculate together as to what it all means, but simply cannot come up with an answer.

I ask Ramon if he or his fishermen friends have seen the carpenter lately, or, even know where he may be. He says that no one knows, and it's a matter of concern because they miss his wanderings here at the shore. We can only conclude that the carpenter has … gone missing.

Will he come back to Galilee?

MYSTERY

I feel at a loss, at loose ends, like a hound that has lost the scent. I last saw the carpenter more than a week ago at the baptism, after which he walked away, up river, and could not be found.

The Galilean fishermen, when they try to remember, agree that they haven't seen him for at least **three** weeks! They have considered organizing a search party, but have put that off because the fishing is good of late, and they must take advantage of it.

These fishermen find delays to be frustrating. For instance, one fisherman, by the name of Simon, is in a bind because he needs to help care for his ailing mother-in-law.

Other fishermen are conflicted too, in one way or another. Zebedee, for one, and his sons, James and John, are plagued with breaks in their old fishing nets, requiring time-consuming mending.

Others have leaking boats, broken or lost oars, or torn sails, all of which cut into their fishing. On top of that, wind and rain are sometimes so strong on the sea that they have to just wait it out.

By now, I've made quite a few friends among these fishermen. They are curious as to what I do for a living, and are amazed that I can get by just by carving engravings in plates and trays that many people are happy to buy.

We often swap stories about our work, enough stories to fill a book, most likely. The fishermen like to talk about the carpenter because he is so unusual in so many ways.

They say his wisdom is remarkable. He can take any common thing, such as a detail of their routine lives; maybe family relations, or cooking, or walking, or fishing, or weather, or just about anything, and turn it into a bigger story with a great meaning.

Clearly, they miss the carpenter. The fishermen promise to be on the lookout, and I promise to ask around as I move about, selling my art.

My art sales are becoming brisk. Some buyers are repeat buyers, intent on developing a set, maybe of animals, like horses, goats, or sheep; or maybe of human figures, or boats. In short, there is more demand for my carvings than I can meet, so I take orders and create a backlog.

With my art as an opening, I visit many homes (not all wealthy, as at first) and meet many people of various classes. I find that awareness of the carpenter is growing. Even people who have known him since his childhood are questioning just who he really is.

Almost everyone I meet who know him, or just know **of** him, are developing theories or questions as to who he is. Many who thought they knew him in years past are not so sure anymore.

They say he attracts people like a lure. He cannot be ignored. But the lad who was unusual, has become a man who is mysterious.

And, now, many aren't sure that they know him at all.

The carpenter is said to have a masterful knowledge of the Torah, the prophets, the Psalms, and Hebrew history. Leading Pharisees seem reluctant to discuss religion with him for his wisdom clearly exceeds their own.

His simple positions may only seem simple until it dawns on listeners that they are very deep. The carpenter can challenge the "men of knowledge" to the point that they become speechless … and awestruck.

Through my art, I have developed contacts, not only in the countryside, but in the towns of Bethaisda, Nazareth, Capernaum, and others. I find interest in the carpenter everywhere I go.

I continue my carving, village visits, house calls, sales, and general conversations. Often the subject turns to the carpenter, and I listen for clues to his whereabouts, but always coming to a dead end … until I revisit my friend, Rebekah, one day.

CHAPTER V
GLIMPSES

SATAN

Today, I'm re-visiting Rebekah, the widow lady I met weeks ago in Nazareth. The carpenter, coincidentally, had dropped in yesterday, just to talk, she says.

To her, the talk was unlike any she had ever had before. The carpenter had always liked her, she said, throughout their former years as neighbors. But this visit was different.

She says, "He wanted to tell me … that he had been tempted by Satan three times, and in three ways, over forty days … and had turned him away each time."

I ask her to tell me about it, everything she can remember from his visit. She seems glad that I ask. I think the account she heard must be so unusual that she really needs to talk about it. We settle into comfortable, upholstered chairs. And she begins, and I quietly listen.

She says: "When my carpenter friend stopped yesterday, it was obvious that he was thoughtful. His smile was soft and his mood was gentle. I can't relate his exact words, but I can give you a summary, more like the crux of what he said."

"These are his words, the best that I remember:"

'Rebekah, some six weeks ago, I was baptized by John in the Jordan River.

'Immediately, I went to the desert wilderness to meditate. For several weeks, I was there. It was then that Satan spoke in my ear.

'He gave me tempting thoughts, three distinct times and in three different ways. Each temptation was to be selfish, one way or another. But each time I turned him away with these responses:

1. Man lives not on bread alone, but on every word from the mouth of God.

2. Do not put the Lord your God to the test.

3. Away from me Satan! I must worship God, and serve him only. *

'I feel different now, Rebekah, like my life is not my own. I'm among people of earth for a crucial purpose, not to be delayed or diverted. I feel compelled to move quickly, even urgently. You'll understand … someday.

*When I ceased my wandering in the desert, I came back to Nazareth. And now here I am, thanking you, Rebekah, for listening. But, now, I must go.' ****

Now, speaking for herself, Rebekah leaning forward, touches my hand, and says: "Caleb, what I've just told you is what the carpenter told me yesterday. It is a compelling account, even if a bit eerie."

To Rebekah, I say: "I think this account will find its place in history!"

We embrace. We are good friends. And I take my leave.

Now I know where the carpenter has been: In the wilderness. But, where will he be next?

*** See Matthew 4:1-11**
**** Author's words in italics, not taken from the Bible.**

100

TEACHER

I'm riding to Capernaum by way of the travel path from Nazareth. Hero has been tethered to a rail most of the afternoon, so he is glad to be on the go again.

As Hero and I move along at a comfortable pace, I review Rebekah's account in my mind. I'm beginning to think this man may really be different from the rest of us. I resolve to regularly visit the places where he has been seen, hoping to learn more, starting tomorrow at the Galilean shore.

After an hour or so of steady travel, Hero seems to recognize the approach to Capernaum, and he steps up his pace a bit. And I'm beginning to think of the pleasures of the inn: good food, good rest, good companionship with both the innkeeper and the guests, and a pleasant home-like atmosphere.

We're finally at the stable where the stable-master greets us warmly. I dismount, remove Hero's saddle and travel pack, rub his big ears, tell him good night, and release him to the care of the stable. I cross the dirt street to the inn where the welcome is warm and a light supper awaits latecomers on a sideboard. The sun is down. The night air feels cool to my skin.

I enjoy a snack from the sideboard, and head upstairs to my room to lie down. Peace, at last. The soft glow of moonlight covers my bed. The window is open. The sweet peace of sleep puts a pause to my conscious thoughts.

I awaken in the predawn of morning, rested and eager to start the day. I freshen up a bit in the darkness and listen for sounds of life in the inn. But I hear nothing. Apparently all are still abed.

I am hungry, so I creep downstairs to the dining area. All is dark. I feel my way to the sideboard, and find some bread and fruit remaining from yesterday. As I stand there, eating yesterday's leftovers, a faint glow in the east emerges dimly to reveal my surroundings, and dawn's promise of a clear sky!

With a new day, I hope to get a closer look at the carpenter. It's early morning now as I walk down the sloping ground to the shore where the fishermen are starting their day.

Over time, they have accepted me as one of their own, though I do not fish. I do, however, offer a hand wherever useful, and they accept happily.

These men are intelligent, but not highly educated. They laugh at danger. I think it's because danger so often springs forth on the Sea of Galilee. Wind storms crop up from nowhere. They come with little warning, and they are violent enough to swamp the boats. When the winds come, the men row hard for the nearest shore. Over the centuries, many boats have gone to the bottom with crewmen tangled in nets and ropes, never to be found.

These fishermen, I notice, are very comradely, laughing and joking together, helping each other, knowing each other's families, their joys and sorrows, and their hopes and dreams. They tend to be superstitious, seeing omens in most everything. Most are tenderhearted, but you learn this only by knowing them well.

On the surface, they bristle with rough edges as seen in their oaths and practical jokes. They almost all speak loudly, a habit formed from the need to talk over the noise of the lapping water and gusty winds. But, they speak loudly everywhere else, as well, due to the habit.

These men have much In common, such as values, beliefs, and devotion to family. But, now-a-days, the greatest thing they have in common is an intense curiosity and interest in the carpenter. They pump me for everything I've heard.

I try my best to relate my Jordan River experience where I saw the carpenter come to John to be baptized. I try to tell them how it felt to be there. The aura and the "other world" feeling is hard to describe. Then I tell them about the carpenter "vanishing" before we knew it, and how a few men searched the area but did not find him.

My friends listen intently as I tell them that weeks went by before the carpenter was seen by anyone, anywhere. Then he briefly re-appeared in Nazareth where my friend, Rebekah, saw him two days ago. Where he is now I don't know.

I assure the fishermen that I've told them everything as accurately as I possibly can. They are puzzled, even dumbfounded, and beg me to tell it all again, so I do. I think they want to hear it more than once to see if I repeat it as I first told it. Finally, they seem satisfied, but they don't understand. I don't understand either.

The fishermen return to their work of prepping and launching their boats. We promise to tell each other right away if any of us hear or see anything of the carpenter.

Word comes one day that the carpenter has been seen walking, not only in Nazareth, but in Capernaum, Bethsaida, and Chorazin as well, and that people are usually along side or trailing, both men and women, and sometimes children.

My friend, Ramon, has seen these walking groups at close range. In fact, he has at times had to move aside to let them pass. The carpenter would nearly always be talking. But when at times the carpenter falls silent, a cacophony of sound erupts from the group as several demand elaboration or continuation of his commentary.

Ramon knows some of the followers, he says. Among them are young men brimming with curiosity, a few middle-age men and some women who give rapt attention to his words, and a few children who seem to love him. Ramon knows that some of the carpenter's followers are well off, or at least have access to money. And they seem to provide for the carpenter as needs arise.

A new name has emerged for the carpenter. Many now call him "teacher." It is said that he has reading and speaking privileges in synagogues in Capernaum and Bethsaida where he astounds the rabbis and congregations with wisdom and knowledge. I, too, begin to think of this man as … the teacher.

CANA

It's time to find new territory for my art sales. Cana is an interesting possibility.

Cana is a small city, resting on hundreds of years of history. In times past, it was a popular stopover for camel caravans going north or south between Egypt and the upper Mediterranean, regularly carrying trade goods in either direction.

Cana was important for that purpose back then, but, as an inland city, it did not survive the eventual growth of maritime shipping along the Mediterranean coast.

Sailing vessels have become reliable and faster than camel caravans. Consequently, Cana has lost the lucrative caravan trade.

Still, in the caravan days a few families grew rich by providing "layover" services such as camel care, rest for men and animals, lodging, food, medicines, bathing and laundry, and re-supply of travel needs. Consequently, Cana and its people, in those days, became wealthy.

As the caravans dwindled, the need for services declined, and so did Cana's economy. But Cana itself still stands as a small, happy, relatively affluent city.

Some of the families of the ancient caravan days left their descendants much of their family wealth. Many of these descendants invested in real estate, and are now landlords profiting from lucrative lease contracts, primarily in agriculture right here in and around the ancient town of Cana.

The people of Cana point with pride to the few among them who are wealthy, enjoying the proximity and social connections with the rich. The wealthy in Cana often give open invitations to special events on their estates, and they always insist that no gifts be brought. Everything will be provided. The people love it.

Furthermore, the wealthiest have formed a collective among themselves, through which they provide for the needy, and even for others, needy or not, who have earned special merit.

It may be said that in Cana social classes are hardly noticed. A local court handles the few disputes. There is almost no rancor anywhere. In other words, the people get along well with one another, and Cana is known as a happy place.

I'm remembering Cana's reputation as I approach the ancient site. Upon entering the city (more of a large village) I find people, in the street and on the walkways, shouting greetings as Hero and I slowly proceed. I soon spot an inn with an adjoining stable. This is where I turn in. This is a good place. I have a good feeling about it.

It is mid-day and the inn is quiet. Activity will pick up when time nears for the evening meal. Two women are cleaning the sleeping quarters, and another is sweeping the general area where groups gather and meals are served. The women are matronly, possibly of the innkeeper's family, or maybe widows.

The innkeeper is a genial sort, and he pegs me as a stranger, which seems to cheer him. He likes to talk; about Cana, its people, and its history. And he is not busy here at mid-day. So we take a seat on a warm sunny bench in front of the inn. I tell him my name is Caleb, and that I live in Capernaum. His name is Josh.

Josh is jolly and a little overweight. His iron gray hair is thinning on top, but it is handsomely matched with a neat beard and mustache, also gray. I soon note that he laughs often, and is quick to smile. And his talk is interesting. Josh is my elder by many years, but that makes no difference. We fall into happy conversation, and while away the hours.

Josh talks of the "ideal" life in Cana, how the rich and the average co-mingle freely, how the poor and needy are cared for in a fair and systematic way by the "collective" of the affluent, how invitations to special occasions are open to everyone, whether family or not, rich or poor, and even to passing strangers.

"In fact," he says, "there is a wedding celebration on the Daniel estate right now. It is in the second day of a week-long party at present. Even you, a stranger, would be welcome," he says. "All are welcome."

In the course of our wide-ranging conversation, Josh learned of my carving talent, and asks if I have a sample to show him. I said I did, and retrieved one from my travel pack that I thought would interest him.

I select a small rectangular tray with a scene carved in it. It depicts a traders' caravan showing six camels and two men, carved in perspective (giving the impression that the caravan is approaching the viewer). This tray measures eight by sixteen inches, and it is highly polished.

We have resumed our positions on the sunny bench, and Josh is inspecting the carving. I watch carefully to measure his interest. I see that his eyes have opened wider and he is holding the piece in various positions. He is scrutinizing the surface, probably looking for flaws, and he comments on the type and quality of wood, and its weight and heft.

At last, Josh asks if I would sell this carving to him. I pretend to ponder for a moment, and then say that maybe we could work out a trade. So, we begin to negotiate. With it all said and done, Josh agrees to introduce me to the master of the Daniel estate, and give me three nights in his inn with all amenities for me and my mule.

After a sumptuous evening meal of lamb chops and a variety of vegetables, fruit, and bread, Josh and I retire to a quiet corner table, away from the dinner patrons, and talk until the others leave or go to their beds. Finally, at a late hour, we turn in for the night.

I must have slept soundly because I wasn't aware of any noise or movement until kitchen sounds reached my ears. I opened my eyes to a gentle gray dawn as I looked through the open window by my bed. I got up promptly, tidied up and dressed, and descended the stairs to the dining table. Josh was there, convivial as ever, greeting the inn patrons at the table.

About an hour after breakfast, Josh and I saddled our animals, his horse and my mule, and set out for the Daniel estate. It was only a couple of miles, but I had my travel pack which was too heavy to carry so far. So we went horseback.

The event being celebrated was a wedding, and the party was about to enter the third day. The estate manager's name is Samuel. He and I take to each other immediately. Hearing of my carvings, Samuel invites me to set up a display table on a perimeter location on the courtyard. I'm laying out my displays as Josh says his goodbyes and heads back to the inn.

Overnight guests are beginning to emerge from the manor. They're milling around the courtyard, talking with each other, and watching the arrival of local residents of all stripes. The host has provided a "master" for everything: one for food and drink (superior wine is a point of pride), one for entertainment, one for housing, and one for special services.

This, the third day of the wedding celebration, begins with the estate owner (grand-master) getting everyone's attention. He begins with a "new-day" greeting to all, and then announcements as to whom to see for any particular question or need.

He made a special point of introducing me as "Caleb the Carver," and he made a general mention of my work. The guests gave me applause in polite acceptance, and some start edging toward my display.

It is not yet mid-day, but the musicians begin playing, and some of the guests are dancing. Food and wine has been placed on a number of tables, and several guests are already sampling. Servants are on hand to keep each table neat and well supplied.

Entertainers: acrobats, jugglers, clowns, mimes, and so forth, begin their routines.

Parties, widely attended in Cana by just anyone, provide a venue for socializing, as much as for honoring the stated purpose; in this case, a wedding.

Some guests come as families, some as groups or clans, some as business people looking for contacts, and some come alone just for the fun. As the day goes on, I sell several carvings. But, in the lulls, I take note of the people. Of the groups, some seem close-knit, not mixing a lot.

One such group, about thirty feet to my left, seems comprised of a motherly lady with some young men (sons?). I notice that they stick close together most of the time. On the other hand, various guests saunter over to them, greet and soon move on.

Within the group, the attractive middle-age lady seems more inclined than the young men to mix with others. She walks gracefully from guests to servants and directors as freely as a bird, and back again to her group. I enjoy watching. It seems that the lady acts almost as the hostess, but she is clearly a guest.

A young couple has just stopped to look at my few remaining carvings. As we chat, I realize that they are the bride and groom, in whose honor this celebration is held. When I ask if they know the group to my left, the bride brightens and says that they are friends of long standing, from Nazareth.

108

I shift my position for a better look, and feel my heart jump as I recognize … the "carpenter," now known to my fishermen friends in Capernaum, as the "teacher."

The young bride tells me that the lady's name is Mary. The group is made up, she says, of the lady (mother of a son in the group), and some of the son's friends. She adds that the son, called Jesus, is a man of wisdom, and some of the guests gather round him to hear his comments. He's always a popular guest, she says.

I congratulate the couple on their marriage, and give them one of my carvings as a wedding gift. It illustrates a couple of lovers sitting by a stream, under a full moon. The bride and groom seem to like the carving, and the groom gives it to a servant for safe keeping.

From the corner of my eye, while talking with the bride and groom, I see Mary and the wine steward in animated conversation. The steward seems terribly agitated. Seeing the troubled steward and the forlorn attending servants, I conclude that the wine is running short. A servant, just coming from the wine cellar, is indicating by his motions that the supply is depleted.

It's funny sometimes, how easy it is to read meaning from body motions. I see Mary trying to calm the steward, and apparently telling him to just wait a minute. She turns and quickly walks to the carpenter (I still call him that).

Now, in a voice that I can hear, she says to her son: "They have no more wine!!" And I hear his reply, with just a touch of irritation: **"Dear woman, why do you involve me? My time has not yet come."** * But Mary, ignoring the question, said to the servants: "Do whatever he tells you!"

Some clay water jars stand nearby. Jesus (the carpenter) tells the

*** See John 2:4**

servants to fill the jars with water, and they do. Then he says: "Now draw some out and take it to the master of the banquet."

The master of the banquet tasted it, paused, and became a picture of relief and pleasure, The water had become wine! But neither he nor the steward knew where it came from.

At this, the master of the banquet calls the bridegroom aside and says, "Everyone brings out the choice wine first, and then the cheaper wine, but you have saved the best till now." Astounded, the bridegroom seems as puzzled as the rest.

I cannot verify the good quality because I do not drink wine. But I can easily see the pleasure among the guests. Of those who know the source, I can only identify the servants who filled the jars with water, the carpenter (Jesus) and his friends, his mother, and, of course, myself.

For the life of me, I can't fathom how this change can happen. It is not consistent with nature or science. I can't wait to talk with my new friend, Josh the innkeeper, tonight. He is thoughtful and studious. I'll see what he thinks.

Later, while I'm riding back to the inn, another question gnaws at me. And the question relates, in a way, to what my friend, Rebekah, told me of the carpenter's time in the wilderness; the key point being that the carpenter had come to "see" that his life and acts were henceforth to be directed only by God.

My question, thinking back to the wedding, is this: Why did the carpenter question his mother's involvement of him? To me, it sounds … almost admonishing.

But, is it? Could it have been that he simply didn't want to be seen as doing his mother's bidding? Only God's?

Back at the inn, Josh and I talk late into the night about the change of water to wine. Every avenue of thought seems to run to only one conclusion.

Something beyond the natural!

Could it be … a miracle?!!

CAPERNAUM

After a restful night at the Cana inn, I dress and ready myself for the day. As I descend the stairs from my room toward the breakfast area, I stop four steps from the bottom, surprised by a group of people standing there with eyes fastened on me.

They've heard! Now, they want to hear it directly from me! They pepper me with questions about the wine: (1) What did I see? (2) Who else saw?, and (3) Details, details, details.

Answers, in one form or another, were: I saw water become wine. The servants who obtained the water also saw it become wine. And the visitors from Nazareth saw the change. As for details, I can't add much.

Finally, the group let me sit down to breakfast, but they still asked questions. At last, I rise from the table to bid all shalom, gather my things, and go to the stable. The crowd follows to watch me saddle Hero and settle my travel pack. I ignore them. I've nothing to add. They will no doubt ponder the issue for years. I mount my mule and ride out.

I know they're still watching (I can feel it) as I leave the stable and ride toward the edge of town to begin my two-hour (if no trouble) trip on the travel path to Capernaum.

Riding along, enjoying peace and quiet at last, I think about Cana. The high point, beyond seeing water changed to wine, was having seen the carpenter once again. It's true, I made no move to interact with him, but what I saw was fascinating. I can't wait to compare notes with my fishermen friends at the Sea of Galilee.

Later, as I ride into Capernaum, Hero picks up the pace and moves without guidance. He knows where he is, and is headed for the stable. We're there in a jiffy. I settle Hero into the hands of the attendant, and remove my saddle and travel pack. I visit a bit with the stable hands, and then head across the hard dirt street to the inn.

Tobias, the innkeeper, greets me warmly, and assures me that my usual room is clean and ready. I take my personal items to it, freshen up a bit, and return to the downstairs public area to visit with Tobias.

We seat ourselves in guest chairs near an open window and begin catching up with one another. He is astounded by my experience in Cana.

Tobias accepts my account as true, but, nevertheless, looks for an explanation … without success. After talking about the event until we are both exhausted, we give up and agree that the change from water to wine must be a miracle. Miracles are beyond natural understanding and sometimes mysterious. In the change of water to wine, Tobias and I agree that we may know the truth someday, or maybe not, but for now we'll just accept the phenomenon as a fact brought about by the carpenter.

Later, after our evening meal, night falls upon Galilee, and both land and sea take on a quietness that promises welcome rest. The inn is closed and dark. Most occupants are sleeping.

Tobias and I saunter to the rear patio behind the inn to relax a bit. We sit in wooden chairs, in the flickering light of three oil lamps, and just let our thoughts take voice. Our speech is calm. Silent pauses, normal among friends, are welcome breaks in our musings.

We share thoughts on the city of Capernaum, an aging city, perched on the shore of the Sea of Galilee. Regional trade is steady. The Sea of Galilee is large for an inland sea, several miles, shore to shore, in any direction. It is blessed with an abundance of fish, to be caught, cooked, and eaten fresh, or preserved in salt for later sale.

But buyers don't often come from distant lands. Most buyers are local merchants of the Galilee region. Consequently, trade and traders of the region remain quite provincial in culture and habits. Therefore, local Galilean culture is little changed from generations past, not even altered by the scattered presence of Roman occupiers.

A hint of this unchanged culture can be seen in the unique dialect in the Hebrew language of the Galileans. It seems archaic to the city folk of Jerusalem, far to the south, who consider the Galilean speech to be humorous.

Tobias and I soon get around to the present day, which brings us back to the carpenter. Tobias hears, from guests of the inn, talk about the curious man. He is so unusual, they say. Hard to figure out. Seems to know so much for a man so young. Sometimes he is warm and friendly; at other times, in another world.

Curiously, he is attracting a natural following of men, and women too. But he is not recruiting. No. They search him out. Growing groups of people of various sorts, rich and poor, stroll along the shore with him. They seem to soak up his words, like treasures. Bystanders watch from a distance, and talk about him among themselves, often at the inn.

I'm yawning by now. It's been a long day. Tobias snuffs the lamps. We go to our separate quarters, seeking sleep for the balance of the night.

It seems no time 'til I hear kitchen sounds. I jump up, eager for the day. I feel so rested and refreshed this morning. Breakfast is a delight, the cook is happy, and the guests seem eager to be about their business, and so am I.

Dressed again in workers' clothes, I'm walking down the slope from the inn to the shore. The first friend I see is Ramon, sitting in his boat, fiddling with his old nets. Ramon lives alone, except for his faithful dog, Rio. Ramon and Rio are both aging well, though now a little stiff, both of them. Rio probably weighs a hundred pounds. Ramon, himself, may weigh one forty.

He is a little bent now, Ramon, that is (he must have once stood erect). He probably stands at about five foot-plus, but if he could straighten his spine, he would probably be five, seven or eight. His skin is craggy and more brown than tan, a mark of life on the Galilee Sea. His teeth are gone, but his smile is as warm as sunshine. His hair is thin, wispy and gray. Ramon has become my best friend among the fishermen.

Ramon is privy to all the shore line gossip. He is loved by everyone, and his buddies always include him in their rambling thoughts and juicy tidbits. To me, Ramon is a fount of knowledge, especially of current happenings.

And, yes, Ramon and his friends have seen the carpenter twice in the week that I've been away to Cana. Both times, the carpenter and several people, unknown to Ramon, were strolling the beach, talking. The group did not stop to visit with any of the fishermen, just kept walking and talking.

I find Ramon's comments interesting, and maybe new in the sense that the carpenter seems to have a following. Beyond that, I've learned nothing more. I tell Ramon of my visit to Cana, and the water to wine miracle (I'm convinced now that it was a miracle). Ramon cannot believe it. Still, he is in awe. He's shaking his head as I give him a pat on the shoulder, and take my leave.

I go to my rented work place in the stable to spend the rest of the day carving. That is, until I begin to feel hungry. I look outside the stable and note the shadows are growing long. It's time to go to the inn, or I will miss the evening meal.

Two new guests have checked into the inn. They are traders, I learn, looking for opportunities. That day they encountered

114

a sizable group of people on the outskirts of Capernaum. Deciding to investigate, they discovered people listening to a man that some called "carpenter." He was telling stories, with a mysterious element to be sorted out by his listeners. Then, abruptly, the man bade farewell, and departed.

After the meal, I start walking the streets, and soon enough I find a group, his group. They surround the carpenter. I edge into the fringe and linger for a time. Among other things, I learn that the carpenter is intent on going to Jerusalem for the upcoming Passover.

I decide to go too. But it's getting late today, so I'll rest tonight and leave at daybreak tomorrow.

At the early dawning, I saddle Hero, and head for Jerusalem, expecting to be there before the carpenter arrives. I hope to see him in the urban religious setting which is very different from the quieter life in the region of Galilee.

I'll go to the Temple grounds early and mingle with the crowd while I wait for the carpenter's arrival.

FIGHTERS

Call it intuition, or whatever, but I have a nagging feeling that something frightful is about to happen when least expected … maybe something dangerous.

But what, when, and where? Or, will nothing unusual happen at all? Still, the feeling just won't go away. I can't shake it, but I refuse to dwell on it. I seek relief by concentrating on my travel plans.

I prepay my room at the inn for another month, and my stable stalls across the street as well, in order to hold these for my return (one stall for Hero, and another for my carving place). I saddle Hero, and equip myself with provisions for both of us. I bid my friends shalom, and set out for Jerusalem, armed as usual with dagger and sword.

Traveling alone is dangerous, but I am still young, well armed and alert. I breath the "air of change." I feel good. Hero is stepping along at a crisp walk. The day is dry, warm, and sunny. I'm tempted to relax my caution, but I don't dare.

Shortly after mid-day, I rein in at a small cluster of cedar trees to rest Hero and stretch my legs. The trees are old, stunted and bent, revealing a history of meager ground water and years of strong winds. But there are scattered patches of shade. Crumbled stonework nearby reveals an old well. I drop a pebble in it but there is no splash. The well is dry. There is no sign of anyone around. No dwellings in sight either. There are no sounds of habitation: no hammering, or sawing, no voices or animal sounds, not even dogs.

I pour a little water for Hero from my travel pack and take a few swallows for myself. Somewhat rested, I close the pack, remount, and continue toward Jerusalem.

Before long, my mule and I soon notice a change in the air, perhaps a coming storm. We trot on until I spot what appears to be a cave opening and decide to investigate. If the cave has enough head room we may enter to take shelter from the coming storm. We may even spend the night in it. The storm clouds are becoming ominous. They seem to stretch from horizon to horizon, left and right. It looks to be a major storm. I hope the cave will be a safe retreat.

Hero and I approach the cave cautiously. I dismount and lead him by the halter. The cave entrance is about six feet high, and three or four feet wide. It is dry. The sides are rough, and the top is arched. I enter and immediately note the coolness. Natural light extends in from the opening, but it fades gradually to darkness in about thirty feet.

I lead Hero just inside the entrance and tether him to a large stone. The storm is not on us yet, but it's coming. Looking outside, I find some dry splintery wood (probably pine), and a few larger pieces of broken limbs. I take these inside and shave the splintery wood into a feathery lump. With little pieces of flint and iron from my travel pack, I strike sparks until the lump takes life as a small flame. I slowly feed this with larger pieces until I have a sustainable fire about ten feet in from the cave opening.

With my dagger, I create several splits lengthwise in one end of a dry broken limb. Touching the split end to the fire, I now have a torch of sorts which should give a little light for ten or fifteen minutes before going out. If I could soak the torch in tar pitch, I would have light for maybe two hours, but no pitch is available.

With my makeshift torch, I advance cautiously deeper into the cave. Soon, I come upon a natural recess off to my right. A foreign object is lying there. Is it alive? I unsheathe my sword and approach gingerly. My light is dim, but I see neither head nor tail. I touch it with the tip of my sword. No reaction. No sound. No motion either.

Getting closer with my flickering torch, I see that it's an animal skin, hair side up. I pull it away, exposing a cache of swords and spears. They've been coated with some kind of oil. They appear rust-free. The armaments are in good condition, due largely to the dryness of the cave.

These warrior implements have obviously been hidden, but by whom? My torch is down to a hot ember. I can barely see. I feel my way back toward Hero and the cave opening.

As I reach the point where I see weak afternoon light marking the cave entrance, I hear nervous voices, and a donkey braying, outside. Hero is uneasy. He's tugging at his tether. I throw down my torch and stomp out the embers. My fire near the entrance is still burning. I still hear voices, but they are softer, like cautious whispers.

I take my dagger in my left hand, and my sword in my right. I stand stock still against a side wall of the cave, in darkness, and wait. It's quiet. Are they bandits? If so, I think they would have horses, not donkeys. Then, who are they?

Outside, there is still a little daylight, but it's starting to rain, hard. I shout, "Hello!" Nothing. I wait a little, then shout again, This time I get an answer. A voice says loudly, "Come out!" I wait.

The voice asks, "How many are you?" "Five," I say (a lie, meant to intimidate). The voice asks, "How many mules?" A good question, because only one mule could be seen; Hero is still tethered just inside the cave entrance.

I don't answer, but I ask a question. "How many are you?" The voice says "ten." I say, "I hear the sound of donkeys. Why not horses? Are you on foot?" No answer.

I think the "voice" is bluffing. I start edging toward the entrance, about thirty feet ahead. The outsiders come into sight: two young men and three loaded donkeys. I'm ready with dagger and sword. The outsiders are unarmed. It's raining hard now.

I smile and call out, "I won't hurt you. Come to the fire. Get out of the rain." They don't answer, but they begin tying their donkeys outside, knowing the creatures can tolerate the rain. One of the young men asks, "Where are the other four?" I don't answer, but ask a question of my own: "Where are the other eight?" We all chuckle.

The three of us, smiling now, are standing by the fire. I add a few more dry sticks to liven the flames. The warmth feels good, especially to the two young men, now soaked to the skin. I soon learn that the spokesman of the two is called Simon, and the other is Seth, but I wonder if these are their true names. They are probably responsible for the weapons hidden here in the cave, but this has not been mentioned.

Simon asks, "Why are you here?" I tell him, "I'm traveling from

Capernaum to Jerusalem. Seeing a storm forming, I noticed this cave entrance and decided to take cover in it."

Then I ask, "Why are you here, with three loaded donkeys, no less?" Neither man answers. They see my holstered sword. Simon asks, "Where did you get the sword?" "I bought it in Jerusalem," I say.

They can see that I am Hebrew, and certainly not Roman. My mule, my clothes, and my native speech, attest that I am not one of the Roman occupiers. The three of us begin to relax a little. None of us are too sure we're hearing the truth. After a time of silence, Simon asks, "Have you heard of the Zealots?"

I begin to suspect the truth, and admit that I've heard of the movement, a loose federation of Hebrews dedicated to the forceful removal of the Roman occupiers from our native soil, and from all of the eastern Mediterranean lands.

Simon and Seth tell me proudly that they are part of the Zealot resistance. At this point, I tell them that I've explored part of the cave, and found the weapons. But I assure them that the weapons I carry are truly my own.

Simon says, "Swords and spears are hidden in various locations to use if an opportunity occurs for close combat with the Romans. Other locations hold bows and arrows for striking distant targets."

He goes on to say, "Our force is too small for open field warfare, so, at present, we are limited to small hit-and-run attacks, or sabotage.

Our goal is to rid our land of the Roman occupiers, both military and administrative, and especially of the collaborating Hebrew tax collectors who funnel so much of our wealth back to Rome.

I tell Simon and Seth that I'm going to Jerusalem, hoping to observe a man of Galilee, simply known as the teacher. They've heard of him, as have many others by now, all the way from Cana to Jerusalem.

Simon's hometown is Cana, of all places, and he's heard of the miracle; that is, turning water to wine. Further, he's heard that the teacher often speaks of a new kingdom, one to come. He wonders if this "teacher" may also be a "zealot."

Simon decides to go to Jerusalem too, just to see the man. He will leave here the day after tomorrow, traveling by foot. From here, he might make it in two long days. Seth will stay at the cave to deposit the additional weapons from the donkey packs, and to re-oil the whole lot. Traveling separately, I will leave in the morning and be in Jerusalem by tomorrow evening, well ahead of Simon.

We're more at ease with each other now. The rain has slowed and night has fallen. I find a better place outside for Hero, giving him a longer tether. I feed him some oats and give him some rain water from a cavity in a rock.

We three try to get some sleep while waiting for morning. I sleep fitfully, still not fully trusting the others. Simon and Seth take turns on watch, not fully trusting me either.

FURY

Finally, with the dawning, I saddle Hero and attach my travel pack, and set off. I did not disturb my companions, now both sleeping. Hero seems stiff. But when the sun is fully up, he becomes his more lively self.

We're making good time. The miles slide by. Judging by the sun, it's just past mid-day, and I'm entering Jerusalem already, through a north gate of the city wall. I'm going to the public stalls once run by Dan and his wife, Leah. I'm remembering the many years that I lived with them and their son, Reuben.
Reuben was my best friend at the time. You may remember that

120

Dan died shortly before I moved away, and their only other son, the eldest, a seafarer named Nathan, was coming home to run the stable business. He's probably there now.

I arrive to a warm welcome from Leah and Reuben, but Nathan seems reserved and a little distant. Nathan is jealous of me, I think, because Leah and Reuben have spoken so well of me since I left. Nathan offered a stall for Hero, and a spot for me to sleep in the hay … at an exorbitant fee … to the embarrassment of Leah and Reuben.

I happily accept the stable accommodations. I have little choice because Jerusalem is overwhelmed with visitors, swelling the normal population three or four times over. I'm sure the inns are filled.

The major Passover celebration at the Temple is two days off. Without bothering Leah's household on this new day, I leave the stable where I had slept, and venture into the streets. I walk because the streets are too crowded to ride Hero. Besides, he can use some rest. I visit some of my favorite vendors, those still here, and look for familiar faces among the crowd. The city stretches maybe a mile north to south, and half that east to west.

I meet by chance some old acquaintances. None want to talk long because of the strong air of excitement, and so I keep moving. I visit for a while with the gold vendor where once I bought a gold neck chain for the pendant my little sister, Ruthie, made for me when we were children. I still wear the pendant. The vendor was so busy with customers that even he had little time to talk.

For the most part, my pleasure rested in experiencing for two days the familiar sounds and smells of the city, including the aromas from numerous food vendors. I can see that Jerusalem has changed from the time that I lived and worked here. It seems to have become more commercial, but that may be partly due to this annual celebration.

Finally, the big day is here! The day for offerings and celebrations at the Temple has arrived; a day of excitement for all sorts: pious, old, young, rich, poor, notables, beggars, and thieves. Notable Pharisees are milling through the growing crowd to monitor impromptu speakers, activities, and general crowd behavior.

The Temple grounds are huge. I feel the excitement as I enter the walled area. The actual Temple is situated within these grounds. On the grounds, rabbis and others are speaking to small groups, groups that seem to just float around from one speaker to another. Composition of each group is mixed, and constantly reforming. The cacophony of voices remind me of a hum, seasoned with a variety of animal and bird sounds.

Along the inner border of the walls of the Temple grounds, numerous tables and pens are in place, pens and cages for animals and birds, and corresponding tables manned by priests. The priests sell a chosen animal (such as a lamb, or even a calf), or a bird (such as a dove or a sparrow) to be used as a sacrificial offering to God. The animals and birds are priced at various levels.

The pious can go to a money changer to convert his or her money to the precise coin for an intended purchase. The purchased creature is set aside in a separate pen or cage, to be used in future days as a sacrifice. Obviously, all animals and birds can not all be sacrificed the same day because of the considerable number of creatures and the crowded conditions.

I'm standing alone in a quieter spot, watching everything, especially watching entrances, for the teacher from Galilee. About mid-day, to my delight, I notice him and three companions entering the Temple grounds through a door in the encircling wall from the street. I can see him looking around, apparently studying the crowd.

The teacher begins talking to his companions (disciples maybe?), facing them as though he was imparting some bit of wisdom. When this was noticed by a few bystanders, they took positions where they could hear his words. The little group became

122

larger until fifteen or twenty people were listening to him. This continued for an hour or so, with listeners coming and going, asking questions, and having earnest dialogue.

Suddenly the teacher, ignoring his growing audience, walked briskly to a nearby canopy where strong cords were suspended from its border. He snatched three or four of the cords, wound them into a whip, and angrily lashed the nearest priests manning a money changers table. He grabbed the table edge and flipped it over with such force that it slid several feet on the tiled floor. His arms were flailing, the whip was flashing, he was moving with long strides, almost running from table to table.

Moving like a whirlwind without pause, he continued whipping the table-tenders of the long row of tables, upending them and spilling everything to the ground (money and all). In amazement, I watch the teacher move briskly, his garments swirling, his whip snapping, until he reached two priests selling doves. He stopped suddenly. The entire courtyard was shocked into silence, into which the teacher shouted loudly, **"Get these out of here! How dare you turn my Father's house into a market?"** *

The silence held. The teacher stood still. Slowly, some of the Pharisees approached the teacher and demanded, "What is your authority?" To which he responded, **"Destroy this temple, and I will raise it again in three days."** * Then he walked away.

No one understands. Neither do I. But I know what the teacher said. It was clear enough, and I will remember his words. I will also remember the wreckage.

I have never before seen, in any one man, such ... FURY

Historians will certainly record the event for the ages.

I walk to the stable to get Hero and say goodbye to Reuben and Leah. Nathan is nowhere to be seen.

*** See John 2:14-22**

With a lot to think about, I leave Jerusalem.

CHAPTER VI
MORTAL DANGER

REJECTED

It's just after mid-day as I leave the turmoil of Jerusalem (especially the Temple grounds) and head north toward Capernaum. I make it to an inn just south of Samaria before sundown. They have plenty of room. Most travelers are still in Jerusalem for Passover, and the inns on the travel paths have plenty of vacancies.

My mind is busy replaying the teacher's fury earlier today, and his declaration that if the Temple were to be destroyed, he could rebuild it in three days. I remember shouts from the crowd at that point, and harsh words flying through the air: crazy, mad, delusional, irrational, and worse.

But I believe something more was meant by the teacher. In quieter places like those up north in Galilee, he often tells stories with hidden meanings, challenging his listeners to figure it out. Could that be true here? Do his words mean more than the obvious? My guess is … yes.

I take a cot in this wayside inn, but I don't sleep or eat well. After a fitful night, I'm up before anyone else. I grab some bread and dried fruit from a side table, saddle Hero, and head north. The weather is mild. This stretch of travel should be pleasant.

Taking a break late in the morning, I stop at the town well in Samaria to rest a little before continuing on. There are no reports of danger on the travel path according to the local men. So I remount and move on.

Hours later, I see Capernaum ahead. Hero does too. We're glad to be "home." I leave Hero at the stable, cross the street, and find Tobias, the innkeeper. We sit and talk. He can't believe my story at first, but finally does after questioning me intently.

The man we know as the carpenter, or teacher, seems gentle by reputation around the Sea of Galilee where we are. Can it really be, that he wrecked the arrangements at the temple grounds, and lashed the sellers of sacrificial animals, and the money changers? This will alter his reputation, for sure, as soon as the word gets around.

I take the next few days to carve, and to walk along the Galilee shore. Both are restful. I need that. I find it restorative, and the days pass quietly.

I've been back here in Capernaum a week now, and have settled once again into my former routine of walking, carving, and seeing my friends, and others. The evening meals at the inn are a high point of my day, mainly because of conversations with the newest travelers, and rest after a steady day of work.

Today, it's about two hours before sunset, and I'm just sitting down to the inn's dinner table when a hired runner rushes in, a little sweaty, and tells the innkeeper (Tobias), loudly, that he has a message for a man named "Caleb." Tobias brings the runner to me and says: "This is Caleb. Give him the message."

I suddenly feel a jolt of adrenaline! Could this be connected to father's unpaid taxes of a decade ago? The debt could fall to me! I created a false identity long ago ("Caleb" is not my given name); Could my secret have been discovered?

I have no choice, so I accept the roll of parchment. As I unroll it, I learn the runner is a young lad by the name of Peliel, and that he has carried the message from a lady of Nazareth by the name of Rebekah. My tension ebbs away, and I begin to read.

I borrow an ink cup and a stylus from Tobias, find a blank space on Rebekah's parchment, and write:

I reward Peliel generously and urge him to stay here at the inn until morning because the danger of bandits increases in the night. He agrees, and I arrange a sleeping mat for him. The inn's cook gives Peliel a plate of food, and he retires for the night.

At the morning breakfast table, there's no sign of Peliel. He probably left at first light.

It is finally Friday, and I'm saddling Hero for the trip to Nazareth. We've heard reports of bandits in the area, but I have my dagger and sword, and intend to stay alert along the way. Time passes quickly, probably because my mind is racing in anticipation of Sabbath tomorrow.

When I arrive at Rebekah's home, I make friends right away with her brother, Mica, and his wife, Neva. Mica wants to hear my story of the Cana miracle, so we retire to talk for an hour or two.

Mica had not been to the wedding party, so he's only heard

talk from those who had. Yet, he is curious enough that he and his wife want to see and hear the carpenter, in person. That, of course, is why they are here as fellow guests of Rebekah.

My experience on the temple grounds in Jerusalem is still fresh in my mind. The teacher's behavior there was so out of character with the same gentle person of Galilee that I'm reluctant to bring it up. Maybe later, but not now.

At sundown we go through our Sabbath eve rituals, and retire early.

At last, the special day has arrived. As we approach and enter the synagogue, Rebekah introduces the three of us to many of her friends. The ritual readings by the rabbi, and music by the cantor, are done before Jesus, the native son, is invited to speak. Everyone waits eagerly to hear him.

His reputation, developed mostly around Capernaum, has reached the ears of the Nazarenes. They expect something impressive, but they don't know what. The very air seems charged with energy, with power, with drama. The carpenter (as I still think of him) rises to his feet and calls for the scroll of the prophet Isaiah. Unrolling it slowly and carefully, he finds the intended portion, and begins to read, as follows:

"The spirit of the Lord is on me because he has anointed me to preach good news to the poor.

> **He has sent me to proclaim –**
> **freedom for the prisoners**
> **and recovery of sight for the blind,**
> **to release the oppressed,**
> **and to proclaim the year of the Lord's favor."**

He rolls up the scroll, gives it to the attendant, and sits down. All eyes are fastened on him. And now he speaks again, saying:

"Today this scripture is fulfilled in your hearing." *

The congregants can hardly believe what they are hearing. Jesus continues to speak. It's becoming increasingly clear that the carpenter is allowing his hearers to conclude that he claims to be no less than the long awaited Messiah.

He senses, and I do too, that the mood of the group is shifting from adoration to hostility. The leading men of the synagogue are beginning to stir and make a commotion. Someone says loudly: "Who does this man think he is? Isn't this the son of Joseph, the carpenter?"

Another bearded elder shouts: "We've seen him grow up, right here in Nazareth. He is one of us! Just one of us! He came up through childhood here. We've seen his runny noses and skinned knees, and all the rest! His claims here today are audacious and way out of order. This is blasphemous!"

It's getting noisy. Old men, standing now, shouting to each other, something about blasphemy. Their beards quivering, fists and fingers jabbing the air, cloaks and tassels twirling. Women and children retreat to a corner. Mary too, hands over her face, crying. The carpenter's brothers and sisters, those who are here, seem frozen in shock. Joseph, the father, is nowhere to be seen, not by me, anyway.

Hostility grows! The shouts are deafening! I can't hear much of what the carpenter is saying now for the noise, but I do hear this much. He shouts in a loud voice:

"No prophet is accepted in his home town!" *

Elders order strong young men among them to take the carpenter by force to the brow of the high ground upon which Nazareth and its synagogue is built; We, in the congregation, follow. It is

*** See Luke 4:17-21**
*** See Luke 4:24**

just a short way from the synagogue.

The brow marks the rim of a cliff over which a huge vertical drop spells death to anyone falling to the bottom. I see the elders working up what now has become a mob, urging someone, anyone, to push the carpenter to his death.

Some take the dare and turn to commit the murder, but the carpenter is no longer there. And they cannot find him. Apparently, he simply walked away while the mob was working up a frothing frenzy.

Having lost their intended victim, the mob's anger increases even more judging by their roar, but eventually that begins to ebb. Failing to kill Jesus, the leaders, still angry, strongly advise everyone to shun the carpenter if he should ever return to Nazareth.

The hostile group begins to melt away, mostly in small clusters of people, some still talking. Mica and his wife, and Rebekah and I, leave too, to return to Rebekah's home. We walk slowly, looking down to our path; we are silent. I think we all feel sick. I'm sure none of us will ever forget this day.

I wonder if the anger will ever end. Will Mary, Joseph, and their family be shunned, or, perhaps on the other hand, pitied and supported, by the Nazarene people? Only God knows, and only time will tell.

But I'll tell you one thing! I would bet my treasured mule that this incident will somehow be recorded in written history. And the title may be:

"PROPHET REJECTED IN HIS HOMETOWN"

With Rebekah, we sorrowed the rest of the Sabbath, had a little supper, and went to our beds.

I plan to leave Rebekah's home silently at daybreak tomorrow.

Rebekah will understand. I feel a need to be alone. I'll retrieve Hero from the stable and leave early and quietly for an unhurried ride back to Capernaum. I need time to think.

STORM

I did not sleep well. My mind is still troubled this morning. The carpenter was not murdered yesterday, but only because he had disappeared and could not be found by his "would-be" killers. I'm not easily unnerved, but I admit that I'm still shaken by the hostility and near-killing of the carpenter.

I settle my bill with the stable hand (only a lad) as he feeds oats to Hero and gives him water. The lad asks if I'd heard of the ruckus at the synagogue yesterday. I feigned a lack of interest to put a stop to his comments. But, I suppose the word is all over Nazareth already, and will, no doubt, be long discussed, and longer remembered.

Now that Hero has been tended to, I saddle him and ride out through the stable gate, find the street leading to the travel path to Capernaum, and begin my journey at a leisurely walk for my mule. My mind is focused on the carpenter. I ask myself: "What did I learn about him yesterday?" I eventually settle on these conclusions:

* Facing mortal danger, he shows no fear, and remains calm.

* He has a heart for… the poor, the imprisoned, the impaired, and the oppressed.

* He claims Messianic identification by Isaiah, the prophet, centuries ago.

* He proclaims this to be the year of the Lord's favor.

The last point, I presume, implies a special providential blessing, maybe even the idea that he, the carpenter, is the blessing. Is this audacious? Or, is it maybe true?

As I rock to the rhythm of Hero's gait, still thinking of the carpenter, a more profound thought takes shape. From what I saw yesterday, I believe that he has, in his own mind, two forces driving his life. To me, he seems to have:

A clear sense of mission, and a clear sense of destiny.

I cannot guess the mission or the destiny, but I believe, without a doubt, that *he knows* exactly what they are. And I intend to watch. Sooner or later, I'll find out.

Riding on, I notice that the air feels different. I rein Hero in and look around.

Oh no! A storm is coming! Looks like a bad one too!

The sky is darkening fast. I see massive cumulus clouds ahead, not far ahead, maybe a mile. It's getting darker all around me. The clouds are swirling. Even in the dimness, I can see the violence in the clouds. And noise! The noise is getting louder. The core of this storm will be on me and my mule in minutes. It's as dark as dusk. It seems that the sun's warmth of moments ago never existed. It's getting cold. The roar grows louder and louder. Hero is nervous and skittish. I jump down and grab his halter.

Looking hurriedly for safety, I see a shallow gully some fifty yards to the left; no good. And to the right, an outcropping of ledge with a short vertical drop of two or three feet on the lee side; not much better. But beyond that, I see a large boulder; a possibility.

The boulder is roundish, eight or ten feet high, and just a little wider than tall, and the broad side, I think, will face the path of the storm. I grab Hero's halter and head for the lee side of the boulder. I push him up against the boulder, with his right side, front to rear, flat against it. Quickly, I remove the saddle in order to grab the saddle blanket. I drop the saddle to the ground, and drape the blanket over the mule's head, and mine too. He is edgy, but he lets me do it. I'm sure sand, grit and gravel will be whipping through the air. Hopefully, the blanket over our heads will save our eyes and allow us to breath.

I talk the sweetest talk I've ever talked to my mule. His instinct probably tells him to run, but there is no better protection around. The power of the storm is on us now. The wind carries all kinds of debris, but less rain than I had expected. The wind, if it could laugh, would be laughing at us and our boulder. It hammers us in gusts, not just lateral, but up and down in sudden changes. We are being churned. The blanket is beginning to shred. Hero constantly winces and makes mournful sounds. I feel pellets, probably of stone, cutting my legs and hips. I lean against Hero, trying to keep him against the boulder. Without the boulder, we would be swept away and whipped to death.

Will it ever stop!? I'm beginning to think this storm may kill us. I pray for me and my mule that we might survive; nothing more. If all of our gear is destroyed, no matter. Will we live? That's the only thought in my mind. The thrashing goes on, and on, and on. I stop thinking. Just leaning against Hero, hanging onto his harness with one hand, and trying to hold the shredding blanket over our heads with the other. I've tied the blanket in a knot under our chins, but the storm is trying to rip it away. I can't judge time. Minutes seem like hours. The storm still rages. I'm no longer expecting to survive. My mule deserves better. I'm sorry for him. His devotion has come with a heavy price.

Then … it stopped.

Seems so strange. Is it really over? I can't believe it! I don't move for maybe a minute. But now I'm slowly removing the tattered blanket covering our heads. Hero snorts and shifts his body, but he makes no move to get away. I can see the bulk of the storm moving on in the direction from which we came. It's still ripping things apart as it moves away from us. I feel a heavy sorrow for those still in its path.

It's breezy here now but no longer violent. I know that I have bleeding cuts and punctures over much of my body, especially my legs which are exposed below my tunic. But first I want to examine Hero. The right side, against the boulder, is not bad. There are some cuts to his head, but the saddle blanket gave some protection. The rest of his body suffered more. His back and left side were the most exposed. So were his legs. His wounds are numerous. Some are punctures where a stone or something sharp made a direct hit, and whatever it was is probably lodged in his flesh. Other wounds are cuts where some object struck a grazing or glancing blow.

Hero is bleeding, but not apparently from an artery, thankfully. I don't think he will bleed to death, but I worry about a delayed affect from the wounds that he does have. I need to get him to an animal doctor.

Examining my own wounds, I find no pulsing spurts of blood. Therefore, no punctured arteries. But I do have flesh wounds like those of my mule. I'll clean them as soon as I can, and dig out stones or whatever may be buried under my skin.

My saddle and blanket are beyond repair. I'll leave them here to decay. I take Hero's halter in hand and test our ability to walk. We both limp, but can nevertheless move if we don't try to rush. I estimate that we have about two miles to reach the stable in Capernaum. In our condition, this may take an hour or more. We begin our tortuous trek, both of us walking. I wouldn't think of riding my mule in his condition.

We arrive to find the stable still standing. Workers are picking up debris all over Capernaum. Victims are lying in the streets or wandering in a daze. The inn survived. Most structures did, but many were damaged. A few were demolished. Nothing but scrap. Authorities are tending the wounded and collecting the dead, including a number of animals. Leaving Hero with the stable crew, I enter the inn. Tobias and others turn their attention to my wounds. By mid-afternoon I'm feeling better, and thankful to be alive.

I ask Tobias if he knows the status of our fishermen friends. Had they been on the water? Turns out, many had and were fishing when the super squall hit. The boats took a lot of damage. Some sails were ripped to shreds. Hulls cracked. Masts were snapped and many oars were lost. Tobias had heard that Ramon was still missing. It's been six hours now since the storm moved through.*

I'm still shaken by the synagogue debacle yesterday, and the storm today, but I put on some clean clothes and rush down the back slope to the shore. They are about to start a search for Ramon. Simon, an experienced seaman, is organizing the search.

Five boats are seaworthy. Two have working sails. The two with sails will head for the more distant waters, one to the right and one to the left. When they meet, if they haven't found Ramon, they will continue searching in ever tightening circles.

The remaining three boats, depending on oars only, will search closer, one to the right, one to the left, and one straight on.

Gabe, a newer friend, invites me to join him in his boat; no sail, oars only. I take a pair of oars while he takes another. A third man sits in the bow, scanning the waters.

We set out in our assigned direction. We've been rowing about an hour when the lookout shouts: "Object ahead, easy to the right." We alter direction accordingly, and row with new energy. Whatever is ahead is low in the water. We approach our target at a slower pace, and look closely.

It's a boat. It has taken on a great deal of water. The hull is broken. We see the loose plank. Something is moving ahead of the boat, in the water. It's Rio, Ramon's dog! Rio is trying to swim with the bowline clamped in his teeth. Looks like he's trying to tow the boat. A body is sprawled low near the stern, motionless except for an arm hanging over the side, moving rhythmically

* Author's note: Today, in the 21st century, we would call this storm a tornado.

with the rocking motion of the damaged boat. It's Ramon!

We bring our boat alongside the other and tie them together. I slide into Ramon's boat while Gabe drags Rio up into his. Ramon's eyes are closed. Probably a good sign. No death stare, anyway. I crawl through the water-laden boat, now at risk of sinking, and capsizing Gabe's boat in the process.

I must hurry. I'm finally at Ramon's side, calling his name and feeling for a pulse. Nothing. But then I feel at his neck and find a weak pulse, not strong, but steady.

Ramon's eyelids flutter, then open a little. He says, weakly: "Caleb." I say, "don't talk." I quickly check for broken arms or legs. They seem good. I begin the delicate task of shifting Ramon to Gabe's boat. Ramon is able to help a little. Once aboard, we untie our boats and leave Ramon's to sink.

Now, an hour later, we're back on shore. Some of the waiting men carry Ramon to Zebedee's house. Zebedee's wife offers to care for him. We're hopeful for his recovery. When arrangements are agreed on, I head back to the inn, just up the slope. Once there, I collapse, exhausted. The sun is nearly down.

CHAPTER VII
STRUCTURE

DANNY

I decide to go to my workspace in the stable, to carve, and to busy my mind on art. I need to calm my brain, to ease the tension stirring within me. My mind is buzzing with a persistent memory of violence, the near-murder of the carpenter, and the killer storm.

My mule is mending. The stable's animal doctor has removed as much of the debris embedded in Hero's flesh as he possibly could. And he has treated the open cuts on Hero's left side, and is monitoring his overall condition every morning.

I carve, and carve, and carve … trying to clear my mind of the "close calls" of last week. First, the carpenter faced a murderous crowd, and escaped. Then, my mule and I narrowly survived a killer storm. Finally, my friend, Ramon, nearly lost his life on the Sea of Galilee, from the same storm.

This is my ninth day of carving. I carved right on through the Sabbath, not caring about tradition, or what the rabbi may say. I just do what I have to do. I'm feeling much better already, so my self-directed therapy is working. My growing stock of art is now sufficient to allow me some "free" time. I think I'll check on Ramon after lunch. The main course at the inn today is roast chicken, always good.

Only five of us come to the table. Other than me, there is Tobias the innkeeper (rarely dining with the clientele), and three traveling businessmen. One of the travelers had attended synagogue on a recent Sabbath here in Capernaum.

He said that a young man of local fame spoke to the congregation. The traveler does not remember his name, but my spirits lift as I think the Sabbath speaker may have been the carpenter.

"He was impressive," said the traveler. "Knowledgeable, logical, practical, and direct. He commented mostly on Hebrew prophecies and their fulfillment, avowing that they are unfolding even today."

The traveler goes on about the speaker's demeanor: "He seemed so sure, so authoritative, answering questions directly, not with equivocation. He spoke of facts, not opinions. We (the congregation) did not want it to end, but it did when the speaker blessed the congregation and walked out of the synagogue, leaving the listeners wanting more."

"We all wanted more," he continued, "all of us except … the rabbi. The rabbi seemed uncomfortable, judging by his body movements, and he did not thank or praise the speaker at the end. By then, the speaker had departed. Even though I was a visitor," continued our companion, "I sensed strong support among the congregants. It seemed the speaker was known and liked. Clearly, they wanted to hear more." The table conversation fades as the meal comes to an end. Suddenly, my thoughts go to my friend, Ramon. I must see him to ask if he's seen the carpenter lately.

When I go to Zebedee's home to visit Ramon, the recent Sabbath Day speaker is all the talk. Seems that everyone is talking about the carpenter and his amazing ability to cite ancient prophesies, and declare that they are appearing in our world today. "All one has to do is to look," he says. I notice that Zebedee's household now refers to the carpenter as … the "teacher."

Ramon is recovering. He is eating well (so is Rio). And his memory is good. But he is still dizzy when standing. So, mostly, he sits in a chair, or lies on a cot. His boat has not been seen. Probably sunk to join the skeletons on the bottom of the Galilee Sea, 144 feet at its greatest depth.

Ramon isn't thinking much of his future, but others are; He has several offers as helper on other boats, so the prospect of him returning to the sea is good. Ramon doesn't want me to leave. He talks of the sea. Eventually, he falls asleep, and I rise to leave. I wish all well, and return to the inn where I can sit on the rear patio and look at the sea and watch the activity along the shore.

Much of my afternoon has passed. Now it's three hours 'til sundown. The fishermen should be coming in soon. I enjoy watching from the patio as they sort and gut the fish, and salt them down in the usual clay jars. A couple of merchants are standing by at the shore, ready to inspect the catch.

Just as I begin to relax, I catch sight of a group of people slowly walking the shoreline. One person of the group seems to be the hub about which the others mill around, but the whole group moves together, like a flock of sheep. I can make out some of their faces now. And one I'm sure of; I'm sure the "hub" figure is the "teacher." That is how I think of him now: the teacher!

Soon the group breaks up and scatters, as though its purpose has ended, or maybe has just been interrupted to be resumed at another time. I recognize a lad among the disbursing group, an odd jobs worker here at the inn. I'll find him as soon as I can and quiz him about the teacher. But, for now, I return my attention to the men at the shore.

Alone now, the teacher lingers among the fishermen as they arrive with their catches. They and the teacher display acamaraderie that was not evident before. None object when he steps aboard any of the boats and looks at their catch. From my vantage point, on the inn's patio, I can't hear their words, but I detect laughter and friendly touches. No doubt, they have come to know each other as a happy brotherhood of some sort. The teacher is among friends.

Capernaum, as you know, sits on the coast of the Sea of Galilee, but, on the opposite side of the city, away from the sea, there is a mountain reaching some half mile in height. It's a short walk of two or three miles to the foot of the mountain. Animal trails and rocky outcroppings make it possible to climb to places of magnificent views, views of the entire city of Capernaum, and the many miles of the Galilee Sea beyond.

The mountain is host to such trees as oak, acacia, cedar, and to shrubs such as myrrh. In lower areas, fruit trees such as date, fig, and olive, can be found, and the mustard plant too. Flowering plants are abundant in warm, moist, seasons, bringing lively color, and food for nectar-loving birds, bees, and fluttering creatures.

Foxes and wolves live in mountain dens, and other animals too, including various cat-like creatures. Eagles and vultures have their nesting and roosting places there, as well. Snakes live there too, feeding on mice, moles, and other small creatures.

Adventurous people explore the mountain, either alone or with companions. And the mountain attracts the contemplative sort too, some of whom have favorite places on its heights where they can simply be still, and ponder the wonders of God's creation.

Locals just call this mountain … "the mountain." Other mountains have names, but when locals refer to "the mountain," this is the one they mean.

Around the rest of the Sea of Galilee, I have explored the land, and noted much variety in it. There are mountains, but none as impressive as "the mountain." Other than beautiful hills and lesser mountains, grain and pasture lands are plentiful. Fruits and vegetables grow well too, and are consumed fresh in season, or dried for year-round use. All in all, the Galilee region is naturally pleasing and supportive of life.

It's time for the evening meal, and I'm hungry. The odd-jobs boy is standing in a far corner of the room, waiting to be called into service by Tobias, the innkeeper. Soon, he is sent on an errand somewhere. He returns about the time we finish eating, and the staff is preparing for the next day. The guests disappear, leaving me alone with Tobias.

Tobias and I sit down to review our day with each other, as we often do. Finally, I mention his odd-jobs boy, and our conversation turns to him. Tobias begins: "The lad's name is Daniel, better known as Danny. Danny was orphaned three years ago when his parents drowned in the sea under mysterious circumstances.

"His parents had set out in a borrowed boat, rowing to the opposite shore to visit a cousin about five miles across the water. They never arrived, and their bodies were never found. Later, their borrowed boat was found . . . empty. Danny was left alone to fend for himself, so at the age of twelve he became an errand boy and an odd-jobber. Danny more or less came under my wing, but others help him too. He usually sleeps in my storage room, but sometimes he stays for a night or two with other friends," says Tobias.

I tell Tobias that I saw Danny in the crowd with the teacher. "This interests me," I say, "and I might like to hire him as a helper and a consultant, but I'm first asking your permission since he is obligated to you. He could still be available to you. I would gladly pay for his lodging in the inn. He would be primarily available to me, but secondarily, to you." Tobias thinks a moment, then says: "Agreed. if Danny agrees."

We plan for Tobias to discuss the offer with Danny and see if he is interested. If so, Tobias will introduce him to me, and leave the two of us to discuss the offer.

Two days pass before I learn the result, and it turns out that the job is highly attractive to Danny. We agree on a trial period of one month with possible extensions.

The ways of the local population of the Galilee region have not changed much from its ancestral roots. Danny is typical:

intelligent but meagerly schooled, fascinated by anything new or unusual, conversant in the basic idiomatic Hebrew dialect, energetic, admired by his peers, and respected by his elders.

Danny and I discuss our shared interest in the teacher, and how quickly our local people become attracted to him.

The people here are people of the earth, their thoughts guided by what they see and touch. They are not philosophers, and yet they are open to new thoughts. They love stories and story tellers, and are attracted to such people. To them, stories are entertaining. They are quick to gather 'round good story tellers. Danny, being a native son, is a typical Galilean, fitting easily into any local gathering, sometimes hearing the teacher's stories.

Locals say that story telling is where the teacher excels. He captures and holds their attention with good stories. His stories are seasoned with the drama of love, pity, hate, compassion, rescue, fairness, and more. His stories seem complete, but he often ends them with a mysterious challenge: "Figure it out", he says. "The story means more than it seems. See if you can figure it out."

My first assignment for Danny is to join groups when he sees them collecting around the teacher. I tell him to listen to the teacher, but also to keep scanning the group to gauge their mood, and, especially, to note their questions and their attitude toward the teacher. Further, if Danny knows a group is about to form, and can get word to me before the event, he is to let me know. Danny loves this assignment. Away he goes.

TWELVE

Danny is fifteen, lean and healthy. He can run a loping gate for miles without rest, and he can make a quarter mile dash in seconds. Danny is crowned with a mop of very dark hair, usually mussed, exposing the lower portion of his ears and his neck. His complexion is ruddy by nature, and heightened by long outdoor exposure. It has been three years since he lost his parents.

Danny has a keen interest in the teacher. He watches for him, and when he sees him with a trailing group, Danny is quick to join. He watches both the crowd and the teacher, and then reports to me what he has seen and heard.

"The teacher is a superb story teller," Danny says. "His stories are short and gripping, and the teacher often says they have hidden meanings to be figured out." * The challenge, of course, seals the stories in memory.

I tell Danny what I saw in Cana, and later in Nazareth. Danny wants to know every detail. He probes my memory relentlessly. The lad is perceptive far beyond his years. His insightful questions stimulate my thinking. I value Danny more every day. He is younger than I by ten years, but he's becoming a prized companion.

We spend hours talking about the teacher, and the Cana and Nazareth events. We note that the teacher interacted with the public in both instances, but with wildly different reactions. We wonder why, but we let the question rest. And then there is the teacher's fury in Jerusalem; we're astounded and puzzled, but we let that rest too.

Danny and I draw Tobias, the innkeeper, into our conversation one night. While the kitchen and clean-up crew are closing the public area of the inn for the night, we three settle down on the back patio, just to talk and watch a few men on the beach having a simple fish supper around the glowing embers of a small wood fire. Night has fallen.

The men had kept out a few fish of the day's catch, gutted and rinsed them, and suspended them over the embers to roast.

*** "He who has ears to hear, let him hear."**
See Matthew 13:8-10, and others.

When done, we watch them spread them open and peal out the spine and ribs, and begin eating. They dine on their campfire supper with contented sounds. Finally, they douse the fire and go home.

While watching all this, our conversation turns to the teacher. Word around the inn is that he is accompanied by ever larger crowds. Tobias has learned that the teacher not only attracts groups in the open country, but he also speaks in the Capernaum synagogues. Congregations are open to him, but the leaders (mostly Pharisees) are not. The teacher may be appreciated more in Capernaum than anywhere else. He is definitely popular with the common folk.

It has gotten very late, so Tobias, Danny and I, call it a day and go to our beds.

At the dawn of a new day, Danny and I join each other and sit down to a sumptuous breakfast. I tell Danny to keep scouting for the teacher while I return to my carving.

Days pass with no sightings by Danny. My own days have fallen into a routine: eating, sleeping, and carving.

But today, from my stable workshop, I glance through a ventilation opening and see Danny trotting up the street toward the stable. He must have news!

Many of the usual followers of the teacher, he says, are headed for the mountain. Danny had caught up with some of them and learned that someone had spotted the teacher on a rocky outcropping half way up the mountain, and his followers are trying to join him.

"Let's go too," I shout. So we take off. I have some dried fruit which should answer to our hunger later in the day. Otherwise, we go as we are. And we make good time. Danny is as quick as a rabbit, and I am still young enough to keep up with him – for a while at least.

144

By the time we catch up, part way up the mountain, the group is finding places to sit, competing with each other for spots of grass, or maybe a rock, hoping to hear the teacher tell them more stories. Danny and I find places on the fringe, but close enough to hear the teacher. There is little wind, so the hearing should be good and clear.

But . . . there are no stories today.

Instead, the teacher says this is a special day. For some time he has been calling all of his followers "disciples," that is, "learners." But today, he informs everyone that twelve of them will become "apostles," that is, "promoters" of him, his teachings, and his purpose.

For a time, they will continue as disciples, but someday, the teacher says, he, himself, will be gone, and that is when the apostolic mantle will fall on the twelve. He is going to introduce the twelve to the rest of us, one by one, so that we will know who they are. He assures us that we are all disciples, but he wants us, and the world, to know the names of each future apostle, each with a future mission greater than any known before. Now we are super attentive! And quiet.

Turns out, none of the twelve are surprised. They had been recruited earlier by the teacher, but no open announcement has been made . . . until now. We wait.

The teacher tells us that the men he will introduce to us will endure unending hardships. They will leave family and homes behind. They will walk hundreds of miles, over and over. They will endure hostility, hungers, homelessness, poverty, and they may even fall into the hands of killing-mobs or executioners.

On the other hand, they will be promoting the Messianic age proclaimed by Isaiah, the prophet, long ago, an age now at hand. He tells us that these are men that many of us know. They live the lives we live. But, as of now, these men are dedicated to the greatest purpose ever.

The teacher is scanning our small crowd. We are silent.

In the momentary quiet, I think of the twelve, yet to be identified, as . . . daring, courageous, driven men, with a mission that may cost them their lives. But they are undoubtedly committed to the purpose, or they would be fleeing without looking back.

Who are they? I wonder. This crowd of one or two hundred is as still as a stone.

Now the teacher presents the first one, having him stand, and then the others, standing in turn, one by one, as they are introduced to the rest of us.

> 1. **Peter -** I know him! So do many in this crowd. But we know him as "Simon," a fisherman on the Sea of Galilee. We know him as a natural leader, the man who organized the search for Ramon after the storm. And as a man who has compassion for the ill, the man who left his work to tend to his ailing mother-in-law. The teacher gave Simon a new name: "Peter," meaning "rock."

> 2. **John** - John was formerly a disciple of John the baptizer. But when Jesus himself (the man I know as the "teacher," the one speaking to us now) was baptized by John the baptizer at the Jordan River, the John now being introduced to us left the baptizer and became a disciple of Jesus (the teacher). He and his brother, James, are fishermen by trade, along with their father, Zebedee, on the Sea of Galilee. They, like Peter, live in Capernaum.

> 3. **James** - Also a fisherman, James is the older brother of John, and a son of Zebedee. They have a fishing partnership with Peter, thereby enjoying mutual support. Like Peter, James lives in Capernaum.

> 4. **Andrew -** Another fisherman. The brother of Peter,

said to have brought Peter to Jesus (the teacher). Their father is Jonas. Andrew also lives in Capernaum.

5. **<u>Philip -</u>** A friend of Peter and Andrew. Philip joined the teacher at the Jordan baptism experience. He is a native of Bethsaida, east of Capernaum, and, like Capernaum, on the Sea of Galilee. I don't know much about Philip, but he has to be familiar with commercial fishing, if not part of it.

6. **<u>Bartholomew</u>** - Judging by the murmur within the crowd, I think this man is not native to the area. I don't know him, but the teacher travels widely in the region, and must have made this selection with good cause.

7. **<u>Thomas -</u>** I don't know Thomas, nor where his home is. Someone whispers that they've heard of him, that he is very practical, likes to know how things happen. A stickler for facts.

8. **<u>Matthew</u>** - This man was a tax collector in Capernaum, authorized as a licensed agent of the Roman occupation. The teacher says that Matthew has given up the lucrative post with a vow to refund anyone that he has overcharged (or cheated). A thought flashes through my mind: could this tax collector be the very one who had sought my father for delinquent taxes those many years ago when I was just a lad?

9. **<u>James</u>** - This "James" is apparently unrelated to the other "James," the brother of John. The father of this one is Alphaeus, but none of us seem to know his occupation or his hometown.

10. **<u>Thaddaeus</u>** - None of us know anything about him, except that he is sometimes called "Jude."

11. **<u>Simon the Zealot -</u>** Said to have a strong religious

drive, was formerly of a group; sometimes called "Zealots." I wonder: could this be the same Simon that I met in the cave on my trip to Jerusalem?

12. **<u>Judas Iscariot</u>** - Comes from a place in the south of Judah. He is said to be capable as a financial agent and ledger keeper.

The teacher faces us again and reiterates the dangerous and harsh life awaiting each of these men. Their Apostleship does not start today, he says, but each of them will instantly answer to my call when I give it. Then, there will be no turning back.

The teacher dismisses us all, telling us that there will be nothing more today. Then he pulls the twelve aside and takes them farther up the mountain.

It is clear that we are not to follow. Slowly, in little clusters of two or three, we begin our descent to the lowland below. Bubbles of conversation spring up throughout the scattering crowd, everyone probably wondering what it all means, and what may come next.

Danny and I are no different. But we agree that something **big** is about to happen in our world.

POWER

My mind is spinning, or so it seems. Not because the teacher named a "select group," nor is it the individuals he named (though I know some of them, personally, and wonder), but because of the rigors the teacher said they would face. His words foretell tragedy. They are seared in my mind. Dangers lie ahead.

Among these men, two or three I count as friends. Those that are fishermen are back at their boats. Why? I thought they would "leave their family and homes." But here they are! I'll send Danny to listen for clues. I wait, and return to my carving.

Now, a day later, Danny is sitting on an inverted empty keg in my work stall in the stable. The pleasant scent of hay, grain, leather, and animals, season the air. The sun is bright outdoors. I'm sitting on my tool box, listening as Danny reports.

Danny spent most of yesterday milling around the boat landings on the Galilee. When any of the fishermen were around, he was on the spot, offering to help with any chores. And he learned a lot. The naming of twelve apostles was all the talk.

All of the Galilee fishermen now hold in awe not only the teacher, but the twelve, as well, especially Peter (new name), James and John, whom they see every day.

There is constant speculation, Danny says, as to what is coming next. No one thinks for a minute that life on and around the Sea of Galilee will remain unchanged. There is an air of anxiety among the men, but the fishing continues.

I send Danny back out among the fishermen with orders to keep a sharp eye and keen ears to the task, and to report anything new to me each evening. A young lad like Danny, I think, will not seem to be prying, not as much as would a grown man like myself. True, some of the men are my friends, but now their status seems different. I want to stand back a little. Danny, at fifteen, is a perfect scout. I continue carving.

For a while, life in Capernaum seems routine, but at the shore a sense of expectancy takes on pregnant proportions. The teacher, with scores of followers, continues to walk the shoreline. Maybe a mile, and then reversing direction, returning. Sometimes the whole group stops walking where most of the boats are. The teacher points to relevant objects while telling stories with hidden meanings, challenging his listeners to "figure it out."

Then, one morning at the shore, Danny sees the "unbelievable."

Danny trots into my workplace near mid-day. He is obviously excited, speaking louder and faster than usual. Breathlessly, he rushes into the telling.

"Caleb," he says, "you won't believe this! The teacher was speaking to maybe two hundred people near the boat launch. The crowd was so big, and a breeze was up, and some of them could not hear the teacher very well.

"So the teacher stepped into Simon's boat, which had just come in from night fishing, and told him to back away from the shore a bit, so he could speak from there. And he spoke for some time. Told several stories. Always challenging the listeners to 'figure out the unspoken meaning.'

"Finally, the teacher ended his stories, and told Simon (whom he called "Peter") to move out to deep water and lower his net. But Simon hesitated and said, 'Master, we've worked hard all night and haven't caught anything. But because you say so, I will let down the nets.' So Simon and a helper deployed the nets.

"They could feel the nets gathering weight. 'Fish! We're filling the nets!' the helper shouted. Simon signaled James and John, his fishing partners, in another boat, to come and help. The three, and their helpers, began transferring fish from the semi-submerged nets, now alongside, into the two boats.

"The fish were so abundant that the boats were soon in danger of sinking. Water was splashing heavily into the boats. The boats were unstable due to the crew's movements and the weight of the fish. But, with hearts pounding, the crews brought both boats to shore. Nearby fishermen gathered to help clean and salt the catch. It was a record catch, never to be forgotten.

"Simon, astounded and overwhelmed, fell at the teacher's feet, and said, "Go away from me, Lord, I am a sinful man!" The teacher replied in a clearly audible voice, '**Don't be afraid. From now on you will catch men. Come, follow me.**' *

*** See Luke 5:10**

"Then, forgetting the great catch of fish, all three, Peter, James, and John, left their boats, gear, and their entire business, with Zebedee, and, followed Jesus."

With this, Danny ended his account, and said once more, "Can you believe it, Caleb!?, you should've seen it!"

Astounded, I see even more than Danny does. I see, in my mind, these disciples walking away with the master, not looking back, leaving family, friends, and possessions behind, and going forth on a dangerous lifetime mission that they can envision only as it unfolds. And they are fully devoted to Jesus.

I finally see that some power, heretofore unheard of in any man, is present in the person of the teacher. Two happenings, I know for sure: changing water to wine, and the enormous catch of fish.

And there are other miraculous happenings, allegedly seen by others. For example, he is said to have fed thousands by miraculously multiplying five loaves and two fish enough to feed five thousand. Astounding! So is his teaching. His followers gain in numbers every day. His reputation is growing and spreading.

He says that he is the Son of God. And now he is gathering his future Apostles. A "new day" is beginning.

This all seems good. The teacher is gaining followers and supporters every day. But he has enemies too, mostly among the religious leaders, primarily the Pharisees. Do you remember their intent to murder him in Nazareth?

Tomorrow, I'll go to Nazareth to see my friend, Rebekah. She has sources different from mine. It's high time we talk again.

CHAPTER VIII
HUNTED

NO-NAME

After a good night's sleep and a breakfast of fish, bread, and fruit, I cross the street to the stable. The stable hands are cheerful, "talking" to the animals. The weather is perfect. Looks like a good day. I tell the hands that I'll be away for three days, more or less, so they will know when to expect me back.

"While I'm away," I tell Danny, "I want you to keep busy scouting the north and west shore of the Sea of Galilee, looking for the teacher, and noting anything unusual."

And I tell him to occasionally patrol the streets of Capernaum, which, of course, is on the shore of the same sea. If he sees any sizable group forming around the teacher, either in the city or on the shore, he is to blend in with them to observe and listen, and report to me when I return from Nazareth.

I saddle Hero, and rub his ears as I put his halter on. I strap on my sword and check my dagger, as I usually do, before traveling the byways alone. Bidding all hands God's peace, Hero and I leave the stable and head for the travel path to Nazareth.

Within a half mile, I come upon a forlorn beggar wearing nothing but rags. He's leaning on a heavy walking stick fashioned from a broken branch of a tree. I pull Hero to a stop beside the beggar and just look at him.

His body looks rather strong, even though his back is bent

forward in a pronounced curve. This apparently prevents him from standing erect. But he gives me a sideways look and tries to smile. His lips are cracked. I see only one dirty tooth. He has abundant facial hair, also dirty.

"What's your name," I ask. "No name," he says, in a raspy voice. I ponder that, then ask, "Where is your home?" He looks at the ground, and says, "nowhere … and everywhere." "Why aren't you in the city?" I ask. He says, "they won't have me." I decide, then, to postpone my trip to Nazareth, and try to help No-name instead.

Turning Hero back toward Capernaum, I tell No-name to hold the stirrup of my saddle. "I'm taking you to the Sea of Galilee. You're going to shed those rags you're wearing, and I'll put you in some good clothes. Then I'll give you a good meal and some money, and find a job for you. "Can you work?" I ask. He says, "I used to break horses to the saddle until I hurt my back."

Finally, we're approaching the shore. At the waters edge, I say to No-name: "Strip naked, get in the water neck deep, duck completely under a few times and scrub yourself clean, including your head and hair." No-name obeys as humbly as a child. Then he asks, "Can I come out now?" "Yes," I say, "come on out and stand in the sun 'til you're dry."

Now my semi-retired fisherman friend, Ramon, comes along to see what's going on. I fill him in and ask him to lead Hero to the stable while I tend to No-name. With that taken care of, I strip off my tunic and my sandals, and give them to No-name. I'm still wearing an undergarment. No-name dons my clothes, and now is dressed better than I am, for I am only wearing my undergarment.

We walk up to the inn, and I ask Tobias to see that this man gets a good meal (something that he can eat without teeth) while I go to my room for another set of clothes. After I return and we've both eaten, I take No-name across the street to the stable. I explain it all to the stable owner, a compassionate man, and he offers No-name a temporary job as a muckraker. This pleases No-name immensely.

I make a place in my rented work stall for No-name to sleep. My tools are locked in a heavy chest, so I know they are safe. And, at least one stable hand is on hand every night. No-name's modest pay as a muckraker will enable him to buy meals, most likely from a street vendor. So now we'll see what happens.

This has taken all day, so I'll wait 'til tomorrow to resume my trip to Nazareth. Danny shows up at the inn in the evening. "Nothing to report," he says. I tell him of finding No-name and where he is and ask Danny to keep a casual eye on him, but be careful not to spook him.

After our evening meal, Danny, Tobias, and I, drift to the back patio to discuss the day. Most of our talk is about No-name, but it is speculation for the most part. None of us have seen or heard of him before. It becomes dusky, and the three of us go to our quarters for the night.

Morning finds me well rested and wondering how No-name made out overnight. Breakfast over, and a new day ahead, I go to the stable to get Hero. No-name is already up and at work. He mucks up the dirty straw and carts it outside to the manure pile. He spreads fresh straw as he gathers the old, thereby keeping all the animals comfortable.

I saddle Hero and head for Nazareth. Arriving before noon with no problems, I quarter my faithful mule in the public stable. After chatting with the stable-master for a while, I walk out to the street, heading to Rebekah's.

She answers the door looking a bit tired, and surprised too, because I had no easy way to tell her in advance of my coming. She had not slept well last night, but she receives my gift of salted fish and a new carving with pleasure. She invites me in.

We go to her little courtyard to the rear of her house because

154

the weather is so perfect. A slight breeze is stirring. Small birds flit in and out of the yard, searching for their favorite snacks of seeds and bugs. The setting is very peaceful.

Rebekah brushes away my apology for dropping in unannounced. She calls me a special friend, and assures me that I am always welcome.

"I have much to tell you," I say. And so the afternoon begins its gentle passing with me telling about the "twelve," and the miracles that I've either observed or been close to.

Then I tell her about No-name, the beggar. She brightens and says, "I've seen a beggar by that description! He's appears here sometimes, like a phantom, appearing, and disappearing, just as quickly. People talk about him, but no one seems to know his name, or anything about him. Probably no one inquires.

"I think the carpenter, or the teacher as you call him, would like your beggar, for he surely loves the poor, the maimed, and the downtrodden. This much I know."

Then, looking toward the ceiling, as if in thought, Rebekah tests my memory.

She asks, "Do you remember his sabbath talk in our Nazareth synagogue on that frightful day some time ago? Because of the threat to his life on that occasion, many may have forgotten his words, but I haven't. They were, first of all, quotes of Isaiah, the prophet. And the teacher claimed to be the subject of Isaiah's quote. The congregation took that to mean . . . Messiah."

"I remember," I say. After a period of silence, I ask, "Do you think we're beginning, at last, to identify the teacher? Do you think he could be a man with . . . no beginning . . . and no ending?"

Rebekah does not answer "yes" or "no." She only remarks that "it's a deep thought!"

"By the way," she says, "we know he has enemies … and so do we, simply by our interest in him." I nod in agreement.

The evening air in Rebekah's courtyard is getting cool, and I rise to take my leave. I tell her that I'll check in to the Nazareth inn for the night, but would like to come back tomorrow to talk further if she doesn't mind.

"Please come early," she says. "I'll be waiting."

"And as you go to the inn, Caleb, please be careful."

DANGER

I check in at the Nazareth inn for the night, posing as a peddler just passing through the area (not exactly true, but close enough). The evening meal proves to be very good, and the cot, in a room with five other cots, is fair. Three other sleepers are in the room. None of us speak, so as not to disturb the others. My sleep is fitful, and morning finally breaks to a drizzly rain. There is very little conversation at breakfast.

Checking out, I begin my walk to Rebekah's, going in a round-about way, hoping not to create local curiosity that might embarrass her. She greeted me warmly, and we soon fall deep in conversation, continuing our thoughts of yesterday. Danger, personal danger, becomes our dominant topic.

Turns out Rebekah has seen the master recently. She said, "He visited his family overnight a few days back, and stopped to see me as he was leaving Nazareth the next morning. He doesn't spend much time in Nazareth, not since the rejection and threat of murder. So, his visits to Nazareth, and his family, are unannounced and inconspicuous." After a thoughtful pause, she said: "He favored me with a brief stop here at my home."

She continues in a dreamy sort of way, "He told me things that at first I found incredulous, but then I thought again. Maybe it's true. He says that God is his father, not symbolically, but factually.

"I remember, many years ago, Caleb, that his mother, Mary, whom I have known since she herself was a young girl, declared most convincingly that she had become pregnant spontaneously, and that an angel told her that the baby was of God and was to be named Jesus.

"This brought skepticism at the time, but that faded with her eventual marriage to Joseph, and even more so with the subsequent births of several other children.

"I no longer question the claim," Rebekah said, "I just take it at face value and have watched the gathering proof over the years. You yourself have seen the carpenter's power over nature: water to wine, and the enormous catch of fish. I expect there will be more proofs. And then there is his teaching, and to perceptive observers, his life and actions really are answering ancient prophecies.

"You and I have both heard reports of his teaching, sometimes clearly stated, and sometimes expressed through stories with meanings to be figured out."

* * * * * *

Rebekah is unloading, claiming that I am the only person with whom she can confide her growing knowledge of the master.

And so she continues: "I'm beginning to see that his recurring theme is 'love:' love God, and love others as much as you love yourself. And do loving deeds. Help the poor, the sick, the underdogs of society, and those who seek God. Be kind.

"But the master (the title she now uses) condemns hypocrisy and all sorts of immorality. He is especially critical of the dominant religious leaders, the Pharisees, who have needlessly burdened the people with arbitrary rules and laws of no significant value.

He is critical of the civil authorities too. And this, more than anything, has put his life in danger."

Rebekah simply needs to express her thoughts.

Thankfully, she values me, not only as a friend, but as a sympathetic listener. And I am glad because much of her knowledge is "first hand" and her conclusions make sense.

Rebekah and I mull over our thoughts for a while. I'm beginning to feel as she does about the claims of the master (my name for him too). In so many words, the master says that he is the Son of God. Many of his followers clearly believe it.

I've noticed that the master is increasingly distancing himself from his birth family. I decide to share this opinion with Rebekah, and to give some examples. This is what I tell her:

"An account recently surfaced saying that the master was teaching and healing several people in a small residence not far from here when his mother and brothers appeared, wanting to see him. But the crowd in the house was packed, shoulder to shoulder, and the family could not push its way in.

"Someone near the door shouted that his mother and brothers were just outside, wanting to see him. The master did not acknowledge their presence, but, astonishingly, declared that those crammed in the house with him were his **"mother, father, brothers, and sisters."** * In other words, it seemed, he declared all people to be his family.

"This is another example of the master distancing himself from the family relationship defined by the familial group with whom he was raised. The first example being at Cana.

"Clearly, the master's birth family harbors the natural instinct of family solidarity and mutual protection, but the master

*** See Matthew 13:46-50**

158

seems to be enlarging the concept of his true family, probably to strengthen his assertion that he is the "Son of God," with kinship to all of mankind."

There is no doubt now, if there ever was, that the religious establishment is afraid of the master. They fear that he may wreck their religious world.

They are not ready to believe the Messiah is here, so they test and challenge him at every turn, trying to prove him to be a fraud. This clearly spells danger for him, and for those who support him.

Rebekah and I agree that we ourselves may be in danger just because of our open-minded interest in the master.

It's past mid-day, and time for me to leave in order to get back to Capernaum before dark. As I bid Rebekah farewell, we promise each other to be careful at all times.

CONFRONTED

Something is odd it seems. I'm walking to the public stable here in Nazareth (it's still a hundred yards off) when I see a small gathering of men just inside the stable gate.

Getting closer, I can see the stable master and four other men that I don't recognize. The stable master, facing the four, is gesturing vigorously. I'm still walking and closing the gap fast. One spots me and they all turn together, facing me. They fan out a little and one of them motions me to keep coming.

The stable master introduces me as Caleb the Carver, resident of Capernaum, on the Sea of Galilee. He then introduces the other four to me: one is the Nazareth city magistrate, and the other three are officials of the Chief Priest's staff, all the way from Jerusalem, eighty miles to the south.

The magistrate informs me that the three staff men are charged with investigating the whereabouts and actions of a carpenter called Jesus, native of Nazareth.

The officials are Pharisees. I can tell by their attire and adornment. They aren't friendly, and I don't like their looks. Two are tall, muscular young men in their prime, maybe in their twenties. They probably function as aides, note-takers, and, most of all, protectors of the leader.

The third official, seeming to be the leader, is older, maybe fifty something. He does not look well. He is slender, and slightly stooped. His wispy hair is graying. His complexion is waxy, and his rheumy eyes are sunken. His nose is long and narrow, and he frequently closes one nostril with a finger, and blows slime from the other onto the ground or stable bedding.

When the leader speaks, his words are punctuated by phlegmey coughs. He looks at me for a few moments. I stand stock still. Then he asks, "why are you here?" I say "I'm hoping to sell some carvings (not exactly true)." He wants to see some, evidently not believing me.

Fortunately, I have three samples in my pack in the stall where Hero is boarded. We go there together, all of us, and I show the leader my work. He harrumphs, and says nothing. All is quiet for a few seconds before the leader turns and starts walking back to the open area, the rest of us trailing. Apparently, he takes my statement as true enough, so I leave my carvings to re-pack later.

I still don't like him, or his companions. The companions remind me of thugs. I would not trust either one. And the leader seems haughty, assuming an air of superiority, often dropping names of important people back in Jerusalem. This, in itself, convinces me that he is an insecure man, burdened with self doubt.

Still, he may be dangerous. His power, temporarily bestowed by the Chief Priest, could entangle me, or anyone, in the ecclesiastical court of the Sanhedrin. So, I'm on alert.

No question, this encounter is about to become an interrogation. I see it coming. I can't simply saddle my mule and ride out because these men represent the Chief Priest.

The leader steadies himself with one hand resting on a post, and looks me in the eye. I return the look and hold the stare … intending to be polite.

Now, another harrumph, and the questions begin, solely to me. The others watch. One of the "thugs" takes notes.

ldr   "Do you know the carpenter in question?"
me   "I've heard of him."

ldr   "Have you **seen** the carpenter?"
me   "I think so, but at a distance."

ldr   "Can you describe him?"
me   "From a distance, I would say he's of average height and weight. The man I've seen, who may be the carpenter, wears typical work clothing, sometimes with a carpenter's apron.

ldr   "Do you know anyone who **does** know the carpenter?"
me   "Possibly."

ldr   "And who might they be?"
me   "Some fishermen on the Sea of Galilee, perhaps."

ldr   "What are their names?"
me   "It's hard to know. Some men go by multiple names. I'm new to the area and don't much try to remember." (somewhat true; silent thought)

ldr   "Have you heard, or do you know, how the carpenter attracts people?"
me   "Sorry, but I really don't know.

ldr   "Are you trying to cooperate with me?"

me   "Yes."

ldr   "Do you know where the carpenter may be found?"
me   "No."

ldr   Another harrumph and a loud slimy nose clearing, then:

        "I think you could be more helpful. (pause) I leave you
        with this simple order, in the name of the Chief Priest: if
        you learn the whereabouts of the carpenter, at any time,
        you are to report it to the nearest synagogue official
        immediately."

me   "I understand." (non-committal, but he doesn't pursue)

* * * * *

The three officials turn and start walking toward the inn without
another word. The magistrate follows.

The stable master and I exchange looks with a sigh of relief.
He says to me, "You did well, Caleb. Rumor has it that your
questioner is a cousin of the Chief Priest. He quizzed me too,
but I told him I know nothing. I just keep my head down and do
my job. He did not question me further. I think he is gullible or
maybe just an incompetent interrogator."

The stable master and I part in friendship. Sort of a "_knowing_"
friendship. We understand each other.

I pack my gear, saddle Hero, and head for Capernaum. I should
be there before dark.

GROWTH

I make the trip from Nazareth to Capernaum without incident.
Along the way, I review in my mind the interrogation that I had
just endured. I find it alarming, not just for me, but much more

162

for the master himself.

The Pharisees are out to get him, and woe to anyone standing in the way. The one bright spot is that the Pharisees seem to fear the master's followers when they're with him in substantial numbers; this according to a rumor heard by Rebekah.

I ride Hero into the Capernaum stable at a fast walk. The stable hands and I greet each other warmly. I leave my mule in their care, and cross the street to the inn, looking for my innkeeper friend, Tobias. It's so good to see him. I feel at home. I'm in time for the evening meal which this day is savory beef stew and fresh bread.

Tobias says that Danny checks in every evening and, apparently, has quite a lot of new information. He's been tracking the master closely, but not obtrusively. In addition to his own observations, Danny learns a great deal by befriending some of the young adults who follow the master more than he does.

Tobias and I agree to collar Danny first thing tomorrow morning to share and consolidate what we have learned. It's late. We're calling it a day. Exhausted, I'm going to my room to try to get some sleep.

It's a dark night. I toss and turn in the blackness. My mind is spinning. I long for dawn, but it's in no hurry. I hope Rebekah is alright. What did the officials do after they quizzed me? Where are they now? Who is next? What is their plan? Are other delegations prowling our region? These questions, and more, fill my mind. I can't sleep.

Finally, at the break of day I'm up, but I don't feel rested. I'm probably bleary-eyed. Maybe breakfast and fresh air will help. I eat and take a short walk, and when I return Tobias and Danny are waiting.

Good friends, they are, one younger, and the other older than I am. We view the present age from different perspectives. But we are honest with each other, and we are compatible, being both curious and perceptive.

We decide to go to the flat roof of the inn for privacy. Once there, Tobias closes the stairwell to all others. We take seats at a small round table in comfortable chairs more or less facing each other. On a portion of the roof stands an open-sided sun-shelter for our comfort when the sun is high or a light rain falls.

From this roof-top retreat, we can gaze over the Sea of Galilee to the east, and admire the magnificent mountain to the west. It is quiet up here, and peaceful.

We agree to take turns telling what we've seen, experienced, or heard from credible sources. Drawing straws, Danny will speak first, me second, and then Tobias.

Somewhere, Danny has learned to speak to the point, and not waste time with extraneous words. Danny says:

> "Crowds following the master increase almost every day, sometimes to a thousand or more.

> "When the master walks, the crowds follow, everyone wanting to be close to him.

> "The master addresses the crowds, always telling stories.

> "Once I saw the master feed thousands of people from one tiny lunch.

> "I've seen him heal the lame and the blind in just an instant, and he has cured insanity too.

> "His twelve disciples/apostles are usually with him. One of them, Peter, proclaims loudly that the master is the Son of the Living God.

"Once the master sent seventy disciples, in pairs, into villages to tell the villagers that he is here to give them eternal life.

"When mockers appear, he puts them down quickly with his wit.

"The master criticizes the harsh rules of the vast religious establishment.

"He declares that he and God are one and the same, just in different forms.

"The master has a consistent theme: love God with all your heart, and love your neighbor as you love yourself."

Danny stops talking for a moment, then says that just now he can think of nothing more. It's my turn, so I begin.

"When the master visits Nazareth, it is usually at night, to see his family or his friend, Rebekah. It is dangerous there for him. His life is at risk wherever he is.

"From distant Jerusalem, the Chief Priest has sent a three-man delegation in search of the master. Yesterday, the delegation was in Nazareth.

"This delegation confronted and thoroughly interrogated me. They know the master is a native of Nazareth, and sometimes is seen there, and here around the Sea of Galilee, as well. I did not give the delegation any names of the master's friends.

"It is possible that other searchers are combing this area.So we should be cautious and reticent around strangers."

"That's all I have at the moment. Your turn, Tobias."

Tobias learns much from patrons of his inn. Now, taking over, his first comment is a shocker: John has been executed.

> "John the baptizer has been beheaded, by order of Herod, during a debaucherious feast given by Herod.
>
> "John was a blood relative to the master through the master's mother.
>
> "The 'locals' are angry about the beheading, and tensions are rising.
>
> "Surprisingly, a Roman soldier reported that the master had healed the son of his commanding officer who is a Roman Centurion and a gentile.
>
> "Reports are that the master socializes with 'sinners' of all stripes; publicans, tax collectors, Roman soldiers, prostitutes, and others."

Tobias, pauses, then says, "that's all I have." He orders a meal brought up to the roof-top for us. We stand and stretch while we wait for it.

We discuss our previous comments as we enjoy a leisurely lunch and dwell on the peaceful scene below: Galilean fishermen, working off-shore and on-shore.

What we see below is probably typical of the same activity through hundreds of years with little change. But now, change is in the air, we all agree. Where it takes us, we do not know.

But we know things cannot remain as they are because the master is in mortal danger. The Pharisees want to be rid of him by whatever means, even murder, preferably in secret, because they fear the master's followers.

Lunch over, we summarize our conclusions, based on our findings to date:

> The master's father is God.

> Access to God is through him, the Son.

> The Son is sympathetic with the poor, lame, misfits, and sinners of all stripes.

> The Son preaches repentance, forgiveness, and eternal life.

> The Son will carry the penalty of repentant sinners on his shoulders.

> The Son has both friends and enemies.

We don't have an action plan. We try, but give up for lack of ideas. So we agree to keep the notes taken today by Tobias, and to be alert to further developments.

At present, that seems all we can do. Our meeting breaks up, and we return to our normal affairs.

As I'm thinking over the day, back in the comfort of my room in the inn, my mind turns to a simple fact; And that is the master's mission, or ministry, or movement (take your pick), is experiencing rapid growth and notice, all this in spite of strong opposition from the Pharisees.

Change is in the air. Will it be gradual, or sudden? How do the Twelve fit in? Will it affect me and my friends?

No answers ... yet.

The public stable here in Capernaum is a place of happiness. It's just across the street from the inn. I go there a lot because Hero is boarded there, and my carving shop is there too, in a rented stall. The stable houses several horses, mules, and donkeys; and two bulls.

Why bulls? Well, some homes keep at least one cow to produce milk, but cannot afford to keep a bull, so they rent breeding service from the stable.

On the other hand, some homes keep goats which produce a different quality of milk. Most of these homes have their own "billy" for breeding. Goats require less space and food than cattle, so a family "billy" (unlike a bull) is both affordable and practical.

From these animals, many families of Capernaum produce milk, butter, and cheese for themselves, and sometimes a surplus for the market.

Very little of anything is wasted. Manure goes to enrich the gardens. Young animals often go to stew pots or roasting pits. This is true also for animals that are too old; their flesh goes to the kitchen and the hides are tanned for leather.

Poultry is plentiful and easy to keep. Chickens and doves are common, constituting most of the meat in everyday diets.

The stable-master is a capable animal doctor. He treated Hero after the deadly storm, probably saving his life. He and I have become close friends. His name is Boaz, named after a line of ancestors dating back to Solomon's day.

The stable hands are a convivial group. Their ages span, I would guess, more than half a century. I know one to be in his early seventies, and another to be about seventeen. The young learn by serving as apprentices to the older.

Under stable rules, bad tempers and fights are banned. If the ban is broken, the culprit is fired, on the spot. All hands are required to be courteous to each other and to all customers, and most of all to treat the animals kindly. Forceful handling of any animal is to be kept to a minimum.

I love the smells of the stable. The dominant scent is of hay and grain which is brought in from the nearby farmland. Straw is used as bedding. It is turned often throughout the day, and replaced frequently. This chore is done by the new muckraker that we call "No-name." He's the beggar that I rescued on the travel path to Nazareth.

Boaz and I are passing some time today in my workspace in the stable. I ask, "How is No-name working out as the new man on the job?" Boaz is delighted with No-name.

"No-name is very good with animals, especially horses," says Boaz. "Even though he is stooped and his body is worn, he handles the animals like an expert. No-name is popular with both stable hands and customers. His crooked smile has a charm of its own, and his bent body draws sympathy from everyone. He is very well liked.

"No-name is still wearing his only set of clothes, those that you gave him," Boaz says. "He is honest. He takes care of his few possessions. On what I pay him, he buys his own food from the local street vendors. I hope to keep him in the crew. The stable hands want him to stay too. He probably will. Where else could he go!?"

"Great," I say. "Wonder if we can polish his dignity a little, as a sort of reward."

Boaz likes the idea, and says he could equip No-name with a set of typical stable clothing. This would give him two sets of clothing, counting the set I gave him. We warm to the idea, and put a plan in motion. We're going to make No-name a new man.

That's it! New man! A new name if he wants it.

"Let's ask him," says Boaz. "Let's see if he would like the name, 'Newman.'" I call for No-name and he shows up in a wink. Turns out he is very very happy with the name "Newman" and with the promise of new stable clothes. He can't stop thanking us. He is so happy. From now on, he is Newman. Boaz will get the word out to the crew.

It's time for me to go on a sales trip. One of the towns I have not visited is Magdala. It's on the west shore of the Sea of Galilee, a few miles south of Capernaum, and two or three miles north of Tiberias, Herod's headquarters.

Magdala is a very old fishing town, possibly older than Capernaum. It is reportedly a town of only two or three hundred people. Most are said to be poor, but a small handful are rumored to be affluent. Those, I hope to contact.

With all my usual travel gear, including dagger and sword, I lead my mule out of the stable and settle in the saddle. We start on a footpath bordering the shore. This is handier than the main travel path for this short trip, and it can be navigated by Hero.

Hero nimbly picks his way through the rocks and stumps of the path with ease. We're breathing in the fresh air, enjoying the scent of numerous wild flowers. So many are in full bloom just now.

In a short time I hear sobbing. Uncontrolled full-blown sobbing, loud sobbing, punctuated by strong gasping inhalations, drawing precious air into exhausted lungs. I halt Hero, and listen. Seems to be to my right, and not far off. I hear no sounds other than sobbing.

I sense that this miserable person (maybe a child) is alone. I dismount, wrap Hero's reins around a limb, and gingerly advance toward the sound. A break in the brush reveals a young girl, maybe eight or ten. Her body is convulsing to the rhythm of her sobs. She is hysterical. She does not see me. Her sobbing drowns out any noise I make.

Ever so slowly, hoping not to scare her, I push enough brush aside for her to see me. But she doesn't see me. Not until I say in a gentle voice, "hello." Her head snaps up and she looks my way, a little to her left. The sobs turn to blubber as she struggles to her feet and tries to run … away from me.

Loping easily after her, I catch and hold her with a hand on each of her upper arms. She's facing away from me. Suddenly she goes limp and would have fallen if not for my grip on her arms. I turn her, pick her up and cradle her like a baby. She has fainted.

Her face is wet with tears, and pink from exertion. Her eyes are closed. Her hair is a dark brown tangled mess. Her tattered dress is filthy. Her feet are bare. She is very thin.

I carry her back to where Hero is tethered, and lay her on soft earth. My water pouch is part of Hero's cargo. From that I sprinkle a few drops on her forehead. Her eyelids flutter, and then open. She tries to move but is too weak. I tell her that I am a friend. And after a time, I think she is convinced, but cautious.

I give her a little food and water from my pack, in small measured amounts. She revives a little, and we begin to talk. She says her name is …"Dummy." By that, I suspect that she is an unwanted child, and maybe mistreated, often or constantly. I tell her that I am Caleb, and that I'll help her if I can.

She says that she has been alone in the family cabin for several days. Her mother, father, older brother, and the dog have disappeared. When she woke up one morning several days ago, they were not there. She was frightened. She called for them, inside and outside, all around. She did this all day long. There was no answer.

As I coax her to tell me more, she says that at the end of the first day, she re-entered the one-room cabin and noticed the food shelf was bare. Food had never been plentiful, but the shelf had never before been completely bare either. Not even a crumb was left.

As darkness fell on her first night alone, she spied a small hunk of bread on the floor, under the shelf, probably dropped accidentally by those who had left her. Dummy (I hate that name) made it last for three days, but has eaten nothing now for the last two days.

She does have drinking water. Dummy collects that from a nearby creek in a clay jar. I learn that water collection had been one of her chores in the past. So was firewood collection from the surrounding woods. She does not know her age, but I estimate about eight years old, the same age of my sister Ruthie when she was kidnapped along with my parents long ago.

The little girl (I can't call her "Dummy" anymore) had, days ago, fallen into despair. This very morning, she tells me, she woke up to spot a large black snake coiled in a corner of the cabin. The family dog was no longer on hand to keep the vile creatures out. My little friend managed to shoo the snake out of the cabin with a stick. But, for how long she wondered.

The child is looking a little better as I slowly give her bits of dried fruit and water. I ask, "Do you mind if I have a look at your cabin?" She doesn't mind, so she and I go to it, about a hundred yards inland. It is just as she said. It has been poorly cared for. It is drafty and dirty. The roof is not sound. From inside, I see daylight here and there. I'm sure now that this little girl has been abandoned, left to face a lonely death.

Back outside now, looking it over, I ask the child, "Do you know what a 'princess' is?" She says, "No." So I tell her that "princess" is a name for a very important lady. "I would like to give you that name. Do you mind?" I ask. She says, "It sounds pretty. Is it nice?" I tell her, "it's a lovely name, and from now on your name is Princess."

"You come with me," I say. "I'll find a good home for you. You must try to forget the one you're leaving." We go back to the lakefront where Hero is patiently waiting. I untether him, put Princess in the saddle, and start leading Hero back to Capernaum. It's not too far. I will walk, holding the reins.

We go to Zebedee's home. His wife is a motherly nurturing woman. She has nursed Ramon back to health after his near drowning. When I explain, she agrees to keep Princess for a month, and then we'll talk. Ramon comes by just now, and when we explain, he offers to pay room and board for Princess. All agree.

Princess seems bewildered, but I'm confident that will change. Zebedee and his wife are loving people.

They miss their sons, James and John, who, with Simon Peter, have gone away with the master. The master has gathered the twelve and disappeared. I leave the little family now to go to the inn for the night. I sleep well, but am glad to see the morning.

It's a new day and I'm re-starting my trip to Magdala. Along the way I stop to look at the abandoned cabin. It hasn't changed. No sign of life. The scoundrels are gone.

Princess does not know the age of her brother. Except that he is older than she. If he is under the thumb of his parents, he may have had no choice but to leave too.

Continuing on, I reach Magdala by mid-morning. I ride slowly through the streets, looking for homes suggesting affluence. I come to a pair standing side by side. Tying Hero to a tree, I approach the front of the first home. I've apparently been seen because a gentleman of means meets me at the door. We greet. I identify myself and tell him I live in Capernaum. This leads to further talk, including my art and my sales.

The man's name is Sandy. He invites me in to show my carvings to his wife and sister-in-law from next door. She's visiting. I hear them talking about the master as I enter. But I tend to business and set up some of my displays on a large bed, a convenient surface. The women look on and begin to show interest in my carvings, but continue to make frequent side comments to each other about the master. The name of Sandy's wife is Tabitha. The other lady is Tabitha's sister. She is a widow, made wealthy by her husband's estate. Her name is Mary. Both sisters look to be in their mid-thirties.

When I tell them of my interest in the master, they take a new interest in me. The art is forgotten. Talk turns to the master.

We talk of our encounters and near-encounters with him. We talk of his message and his followers, The sisters have not only heard of the "twelve," but have met them. The master takes many opportunities to teach important truths to the Twelve, and often allows others to sit in. Mary does so, often.

As Mary enthuses, it becomes clear, in so many words, that she, with money and few responsibilities, helps fund the master and the twelve. Others do too, but Mary seems to be exceptionally generous. She is often with the master and the twelve, along with other supporters of the group. The group travels a lot, walking to places like Tyre, Jerusalem, Bethany, Capernaum, Bethsaida, and more. They walk hundreds of miles.

One of the twelve is the money-keeper for the group. He buys food and supplies for the twelve and the master (thirteen men) to keep them nourished and clothed. Funds are supplied by supporters as gifts. Sometimes the more affluent host the master and some of the group in their homes for meals or lodging.

The master has friends, students (disciples), and devoted followers all over. He has enemies too, mostly Pharisees. I know this, of course, but I let Mary go ahead and tell me. She asks, "Can you imagine the cost to just feed thirteen hungry men, contribute clothing, and sometimes a place of rest?"

"No, I can't. Have you calculated it?" She says, "Yes, the equivalent earnings of six full-time laborers, even though they live frugally." I think Mary has a knack for business.

At this point, Sandy invites me to spend the night with them due to the late hour.

After a wonderful meal, a good night's sleep, and a hearty breakfast, I prepare to return to Capernaum. As thank-you gifts, I present them with four of my finest carvings.

Hero had been quartered in a space behind the house. All his gear had been brought inside the house. Reversing the process, I get Hero ready and head back. I feel blessed with three new friends: Randy, Tabitha, and Mary.

"Mary" is a popular and common name now. When a person of that name is away from their hometown, it is common to associate the name and the town in identification. This town being Magdala, the Mary of the family I've just visited, when out of town is known as Mary Magdalene.

I return to Capernaum to find good reports on Newman the muckraker, and Princess, the rescued little girl. Princess is fitting in nicely with Zebedee and his wife. Ramon is taking special pride in paying Princess's room and board. Not only that, but new clothes as well.

* * * * *

I don't know where the time goes, but another year has gone by, along with adventures like those I've just told you. On at least four occasions, I've dodged Pharisee scouts, out searching for the master. Danny usually spots them and quickly warns me and others.

Times are turbulent because of the tensions associated with the master and the twelve. They're hunted, challenged, tested, and targeted by the master's enemies, the Pharisees.

Passover time is nearing again. The year has sped by. I'm going to visit Rebekah once more, and go on from there to Jerusalem for the celebration. If the master goes too, he may be walking into the jaws of "lions." He is a marked man.

RUTH

With dagger and sword, a week's worth of non-perishable food, and a few carvings, I'm on the way to Jerusalem by way of Nazareth. Hero is glad to be traveling. It isn't long 'till I am nearing Nazareth. Hints of the city are beginning to show: deeper ruts in the travel path, men pulling carts of vegetables, fruits, or firewood, to sell in town, and people, maybe families, walking either to or from the city.

Entering the city, I guide Hero straight to the Nazareth city stable and tell the hands that I want to leave my mule for only two hours. As I remove Hero's gear, I request a complete rub-down for him, and some oats, hay, and water. I want him to be fresh for the trip ahead.

I leave the stable and head for Rebekah's house with a small gift of dried sweet fruit. Rebekah greets me with a hug, and seems happy to see me. She accepts my gift graciously, but she does not seem herself. She seems nervous, maybe worried about something. We sit down and she opens up. She is emotional.

This is her account.

"Thugs from the High Priest's office in Jerusalem are lingering in Nazareth," she says. "They've been here for days, questioning almost everyone about the man called Jesus. They want him. They want to deliver him to the High Priest in Jerusalem, some eighty miles away. He is charged with heresy and blasphemy. His very life is in danger.

"They came to my house, repeatedly, and questioned me for hours. They have heard that I am the master's friend. They think

I should be able to lead them to him. They are relentless, and I'm frightened.

"Peliel, my handy-boy, has moved into the house with me for added security. He sleeps on a cot just outside my bedroom door. So far, the thugs have not bothered me at night. Still, I don't feel at peace anytime." And to me she asks, "What more can I do?"

I compliment Rebeckah on the precautioins she has taken. Beyond that, I suggest that she should be sure the city magistrate is aware of her plight. And if either Peliel or the magistrate could recommend a night watchman for the general property; the house, shed, and all, that may be wise.

I try to comfort my friend by telling her that the search for the master may die down in time. "Try to hold out, and be patient," I tell her. She seemed to feel some better at that. But the most relief probably came from just talking it out.

Reluctantly, I give Rebekah a hug and say goodbye.

I walk to the stable and visit a bit with Rex, the stable master. We talk about the sense of danger in Nazareth these days. All we can do, we agree, is to stay alert for trouble. I ask him to keep an eye on Rebekah, and he readily agrees.

I saddle Hero, add my gear, and head south for Jerusalem. I travel steadily the rest of the day, then make a cold camp for the night, just as my father did long ago. Tonight, I'll sleep under the stars. Finally, I find a suitable place where I can tend to my mule and settle down to rest. As darkness descends, I begin reminiscing about the days of my childhood with my family, and the later years of danger and excitement without them. I drop off to sleep, wondering if they're still alive.

The night passes uneventfully. I break camp and give Hero his morning ration of water and oats, treat myself to a dried fig, and off we go. We arrive in Jerusalem just after noon.

The Jerusalem streets are crowded. Hoping to see Reuben, I dismount and lead Hero slowly to Nathan's stable. Reuben is working in front of the stable. Hero and I stand at the gate until Reuben sees us. His eyes widen, his arms go up, and he yells my name. He rushes to open the stable gate to let us in.

We hug tightly. Bursting emotions stifle our speech. Finally the hug eases, and we both talk on happily. I ask about Nathan and Leah. Reuben, in his halting way, tells me that Nathan has gone back to sea. He just didn't like the stable business.

According to Reuben, Nathan one day informed Leah that the sea was his life, and he was through with the stable. So Nathan walked to Joppa, found his old ship, the Jericho, in port, and re-joined the crew. "We won't see much of him anymore, mother says."

Reuben takes me in the house to greet Leah. She is the picture of surprise and delight at the sight of me, and with whoops of joy she wraps her arms around me and holds me tight. Her welcome is wonderful and much warmer than I expected.

Leah apologizes for Nathan's rude treatment on my last visit. "That's okay," I say, "Reuben told me he went back to sea." "Better for all," she says. "I love him, but he seems born for the sea."

Leah is busy preparing a Seder for today. No guests are expected, just she and Reuben, and now me (newly invited), and a servant woman. Leah has recently purchased a Hebrew slave to serve as a cook and house manager.

This new servant/slave cooks, cleans, purchases supplies, hires temporary help when needed, and in general, sees to the physical well being of the home. She knows how to prepare all Hebrew festival meals, and is treated as one of the family.

Leah estimates her to be in her early twenties. She has prepared most of the Seder meal. Leah has helped her this day, only because the occasion is so special.

The slave's name is Ruth.

CHAPTER IX
IS THIS THE END?

ARRESTED

We sit down at the table for this annual ritual meal. Ruth and I are introduced to each other. Ruth has the ideal demeanor of a slave. She appears polite, even-tempered, subservient, and eager to help. I soon notice that Leah treats this slave as one of the family. She even dines with us at the table. As the meal progresses, Ruth takes care of all the dinner chores, quickly and efficiently, and still has time to enjoy the meal with us.

At the table, she is seated opposite me, and beside Reuben. Leah and I sit on the other side. The meal takes much longer than that of a normal daily meal because of the pauses for elements of the Passover ritual. I frequently catch Ruth looking at me when I happen to glance her way. I start to wonder, "What's her interest?" Otherwise, the meal progresses respectfully, carried along on the rich air of gratitude to God, and a re-telling of our people's history.

The day is late when we finish. Ruth takes care of the clean-up while Leah, Reuben, and I take easier chairs and begin to catch up and reminisce. Leah says that word is spreading of some sort of spontaneous parade this afternoon. It seemed to be coming from the Olive Mountain direction, and into the city.

A long line of people bordered the route, they say. For the most part, they are from outside Jerusalem, it's said, apparently here for Passover. They were shouting words like "Hosanna" and waving palm branches. It was quite noisy, but it only lasted a half hour at the most. Older boys are running the streets with updates on events, hoping to collect coins in the process.

A man some call "carpenter;" others call him "master" or "rabboni," was riding a donkey along the route, they say. He was the center of attention. Aides were with him. Soon he and the aides entered a doorway of a two-story home and disappeared.

Now my heart is thumping. Could this man be my master (I think of him as mine, now)? And who is Ruth? Why does she look at me so much?

Reuben and I step out to the stable to be sure the animals have feed and water. We turn the straw bedding and add some fresh to it. I ask Reuben, "Why was Ruth for sale?"

He has a pretty good idea. He remembers something about an estate sale, involving three or four properties that were consolidated for a common sale just outside one of the city gates. Farm animals and tools, furniture, clothing, and several slaves were on the auction block. He says, "That's where mother found Ruth, but where exactly she comes from, I don't know. Maybe Ruth doesn't even know."

We settle in for the night. Darkness has fallen. Reuben is soon asleep. The house is quiet. I'm unable to sleep, too restless, and finally I give up. So I ease off my cot, dress quietly, and slip out the kitchen door into the cool night air.

There is a strange noise, seeming within the city walls, not far from Leah's stable. Also, I see a deep pink undulating glow, as though flares are sending belches of firelight to the sky. I walk on until I find a storm of commotion in the courtyard of the Antonio Fortress, where Reuben and I had delivered wagon loads of cargo to the Romans some three years back.

Roman soldiers are guarding the courtyard, so I hang well back in the darkness, and watch.

Distance absorbs the yelling and the words, but I can see Pilate on his balcony. His movements show that he is trying to quiet the mob, but nothing works. There is a man standing before Pilate, apparently a prisoner. To my dismay, I recognize the prisoner as the master. I have no doubt. I cannot believe it, but it's true. The noise changes, and a contingent of soldiers and the mob take the prisoner to the street. I follow on a parallel street, watching.

The prisoner is taken across town to Herod's palace. I don't know why. This is not Herod's jurisdiction; it is Pilate's. But soon they all come back to the Antonio Fortress, and Pilate again appears on the balcony.

Off, somewhere, I hear the penetrating crowing of a rooster, the sure sign of first light. The crowing is easily heard over the din of yelling from the courtyard. From the corner of my eye, I see someone running, running away from the mob, and on through a city gate. He's running fast, stumbling, charging on, as though he's fleeing!

I know the body shape! It's familiar! It's Peter!!!

Turning my attention back to the courtyard, there's Pilate, still looking down from the balcony, seeming to be arguing with the mob! He turns to his aides, then to a lady! I think she's his wife! I remember her!

Pilate seems to be facing an agonizing decision! He turns to one aide, then to another! He turns to his wife! He paces the floor! He faces the crowd again!

An aide brings a basin. I see Pilate dipping into the basin and washing his hands in full view of the mob. Then he turns and goes to the inner rooms of the fortress.

Apparently, Pilate has issued an order, I cannot hear it but I do see action. Soldiers leave the Antonio Fortress with the prisoner, the master, in custody. The master seems to be dragging an object hanging over his shoulder. I can't tell what it is. The mob and a number of near-by people follow, many of them women. They leave the city through a near-by gate.

Are they evicting the master from the city? . . . With orders to never return? . . . I wonder!

But, now, I think of Leah, Reuben, and Ruth. I must return to them and apologize for my stealthy absence. I've been away all night, and they have no idea where I am.

When I return, their relief is overwhelming! After fretting and fussing a bit, they forgive me at the first few words of my story. When I tell them a little, they want to know more. We talk about it most of the morning. They had been unaware of the frightening affair. Their only concern was for me when they discovered me missing.

Finally we are left with this question: What happened after the mob and their prisoner passed through the gate this morning and out of the city? Was he set free? Maybe we'll know more tomorrow, the Sabbath.

By now, we are all exhausted; me from my night-long pursuits, and the rest from worrying about my absence.

Our energy fades and we sink into a mode of rest, with hopes to learn more tomorrow.

FINISHED

I saw the master removed from the city early this very morning, and we in Leah's household have heard nothing since. Exhausted, we are just resting, sometimes talking a little. The weather is proving capricious today, at one time very dark, and we all felt a ground tremor at one point. But now, towards day's end, peace has returned.

In the remaining light, Reuben and I go to the stable to care for the animals. This takes a good hour. Not all animals are Leah's. Some are those of travelers, being held in rental stalls. Each is marked with the owner's identification.

The chores done, Reuben and I re-enter the house to enjoy a good supper prepared by Leah and Ruth. They've prepared extra for tomorrow because it's Sabbath, and cooking is forbidden. We eat rather hurriedly so as to include the Sabbath eve rituals before sundown.

Well-fed and sleepy, we're ready for bed. I promise Leah that I won't leave the house tonight as I did last night. The only exception would be some emergency, and, even then, I'll let the household know. Chores done, we go to our quarters for the night.

I drift off to sleep wondering why Ruth is often looking at me. Contrary to the previous night, I sleep soundly. Must have, because it seems just an instant before morning comes with the music of the birds.

The city lies quiet today. This is the Sabbath, and work is restricted. An aura of religious contemplation envelops all of Jerusalem. This day is counted as a day of rest. We decide to skip synagogue today. But I wonder where the master is. Will he dare re-enter the city?

Shops aren't open today, but many people do go to the streets for a Sabbath-day stroll. I'm going to ease in among them to eavesdrop. Maybe I'll hear something.

Leah suggests that I take Ruth along, knowing that, in a meandering crowd, two people together draw less attention than a lone walker, and close-by conversations may be less guarded.

The rest of the household stay behind. The stable must always be attended, especially when travelers have left their own animals there. Reuben tends the stable, and Leah handles any necessary transactions, even on the Sabbath.

It is mid-morning. Ruth and I promise to be back by mid-afternoon. We set out with a small picnic wrapped in a cloth. We find the most crowded streets, and blend in.

It's strange that Leah sends Ruth and me out together with no purpose other than eavesdropping among the crowds. Maybe she thinks Ruth needs a break in household duties, and that as her guardian, I'll be less likely to get in trouble myself.

At any rate, we begin to get acquainted. We're hardly out of sight of Leah's home when Ruth mentions the wooden star on the gold chain around my neck. She says she noticed it when Leah introduced us.

"That star," I say, "is very important to me. I wear it all the time."

"I know it's not proper for me, a slave, to be 'forward' with comments, but would you allow me to ask just one question?"

"Of course. You may ask all the questions you like. In fact, I'd rather you talk with me as a friend, not a slave; especially when the owner/slave protocol isn't required. Leah probably thinks differently, so at home the expected show of deference and manners will be the rule."

"Now, Ruth, what is your question?"

"Where did you get the star?"

Startled, I am jolted as if struck by a hammer. I can't speak. I feel hollow inside, anxious to fill the emptiness with hope where I've had no hope. Do I dare answer?

Ruth and I stop walking. Meandering Sabbath-day strollers drift around us. We turn to face each other and our eyes lock. The gaze holds, and I finally speak.

"The star was a gift, long long ago, given to me by a little girl in a wee small village, so small it had no name. It was in the District of Galilee.

"Now, Ruth, let me ask you a question: Do you, or did you, know your mother and father?"

"Yes. My father was known as Benjamin the carver. I've forgotten mother's name, but I have, in my mind, an image of her."

"Are they, or were they, slaves?"

"Yes." ……..

"Always?"

"No."

"Then how did they, and you, become slaves?"

"Bandits! They took us by force from a travel path when we stopped to rest. My brother escaped, but mother, father, and I, were captured. I think I was eight. The bandits took us a long way on their horses. They released me at a big house. But they continued on with mother and father. That's the last day that I remember seeing them.

"I was made a playmate for a little girl at the big house, and was told to always be kind to her and never cross her. The grown-ups of the house said I was her slave. As the years passed, I came to realize that the owners were rich. Later, for some reason, they became poor. That's when they sold me, now a capable adult servant, to Leah."

Listening to Ruth, I'm reliving that awful day of capture, a day that has haunted my dreams. I'm speechless, just looking into her eyes, no longer noticing the walkers milling around us, all of them oblivious to our emerging discovery.

To Ruth, I was introduced as Caleb just two day's ago. Everyone knows me as Caleb. No one knows me by any other name.

Ruth and I let the minutes slide as we look at each other. At last, finding my voice, I ask, "Do you know my name?"

Another pause, my pulse throbbing. And then, she says, …..

186

"Kirby!"

"Ruthie, we've found each other!! By the grace of God, we've found each other! After all these years, we've found each other! "But Ruthie, I must ask a favor: please call me Caleb, only Caleb, never the other name. It's very important to me. Will you promise?"

Another pause. Then ... "I promise."

We resume our strolling, listening to the conversations around us. We hear words, like "Nazareth, Sanhedrin, Pilate, thieves, Jesus, Aramathia, crucifixion, and more. Hearing the word "crucifixion", we decide to go to the Antonio Fortress where the commotion was two night's ago.

Low and behold, Marco, Pilate's aide, is standing in the portico. Upon recognition, Marco waves to me with a slight motion of his hand. He's in uniform so it's clear to everyone that he is a Roman soldier. We approach and greet him. I introduce Ruth as Leah's slave, then ask "What happened to the man you know as the carpenter from Nazareth?"

"He and two thieves were executed yesterday, just outside the city walls," he says. "The bodies have been removed but the crosses are still there. Come on. I'll show you the place. It'll only take a few minutes." Marco leads the way. He's not on duty, so is free to move about. We go through the city gate, the three of us abreast, Marco in the center.

My head throbs. My throat is dry. The shock, almost too much. Minutes ago I was so happy, having found my sister, Ruthie. Now I'm sick with despair, hearing of the master's death. A cruel killing, it was, too.

A crucifixion! Roman crucifixion! Painful and slow! Public! No dignity! Naked! Consciousness is slow to give up. Death ... the only relief ... at long last ... arrives. That's what a Roman crucifixion is. I've seen it before. We continue walking. I see the crosses. They come into focus. What Ruth thinks, I do not know. But, for me, my imagination puts "bodies" on the crosses, one on each.

Marco says, "the carpenter was nailed to the center cross. Convicted thieves were nailed to the other two crosses, one on the left, and one on the right. Occasionally, pained cries came from the thieves, but I heard none such from the carpenter; only prayers and loving comments. Toward the end, he said, *'it is finished.'"* *

Marco went on, "Many people watched the ordeal, some jeering, some praying, some crying, and some wanting to ease the suffering, but there was no way." Marco's voice seems far away, but he is, in fact, just beside me.

In a daze, I look around. The grass and patches of bare earth are widely trampled. Scraps of discarded or lost food litter the area. Birds are picking at it.

Dried blood stains the crosses. Bits of body waste lay at the base. I imagine the slumped bodies.

I shake my head, look again, and find the crosses bare. My imagination has played tricks. Touching Marco's shoulder, catching his eye, I nod, and turn away.

I take Ruth by the hand, and say, "Lets go back to Leah." Still clutching our uneaten lunch, we walk with trembling legs.

LATER

We're keeping it secret for now, that we're brother and sister. As we walk back to Leah's, I ask Ruth a crucial question: "Do you ever hope to be free, no longer a slave?"

She doesn't answer right away. After a pause, she says,

* See John 19:28-30

I don't know. Most of my life, I've been a slave. I don't know how I would live otherwise. And, Leah seems considerate and reasonable."

"Still," Ruth continues, "she could sell me, or she may die and leave me to be settled as part of her estate. That's what my former owner did."

We continue walking, in silence. I sense that Ruth's mind is turning over the possibilities.

Finally, she says, "It's a moot question anyway. Leah won't give me freedom. She just bought me! And there's no way I could buy my freedom."

"Well, maybe it's not a moot question. If you *were* free, I could help you find work, work that you could walk away from anytime you care to. And you would have some choice of jobs. And you could move freely from place to place.

"You might even work with me or my friends, or be in business for yourself. Think about it. Let me know: yes or no, but keep it quiet. If it's 'yes,' I'll be glad to work on it. It may take some time. And it's better if Leah does not know that we've talked about it. Is it a deal?"

"I'm tempted. Give me time. Whatever you're thinking, would it be legal?"

"Absolutely! Think it over. There isn't much time. If you can let me know tonight or in the morning, I'll set my mind on it, but it will take time, maybe months, or more."

"Wow, this is so hard for me to take in. My head is spinning! Tell you what, this evening at supper, watch for me to nod 'yes' or 'no'. That will be my answer."

"Then, Ruth, I will cough to acknowledge your signal.

"By the way, I'm leaving for Nazareth tomorrow, but I hope to be back here in a month. We'll contrive a way to talk then. Be patient." Again we fall silent. Arriving at Leah's, I drop Ruth, check on Hero, visit with Reuben, and head back to the crucifixion site. At a fast pace, I'm there in twenty minutes. I just want to see if I've missed something. I have about two hours before supper time at Leah's.

Approaching the site, I see a man looking over the grounds. He appears to be pondering something, seems to be concentrating. The crucifixions, three of them, were just yesterday. One victim was the master.

Now the crosses are bare. The mix of observers (haters, followers, kinsmen, gawkers) must have been considerable. The grass is badly crushed and litter is scattered about.

I speak to the man. His name is Curtis. Turns out he is a worker from the Antonio Fortress. Marco has given him orders for tomorrow: clean up the grounds, sift the litter for anything of importance, but leave the crosses for the time being to remind people of the Roman system of capital punishment.

Curtis becomes attentive and deferential when he discovers that I am on good terms with Marco. I learn from him that some crosses are kept ready at the Fortress. When they run low due to overuse or decay, new ones are made.

Crosses consist of an upright member, fourteen feet long, and a cross-member seven feet long. The upright and cross-member are joined by groove and fit, and are fastened with six strong nails. A three foot hole is made in the ground, ready for the upright.

The victim is nailed to the cross while the cross is flat on the ground. Nails engage the tendons in the victim's hands and feet. This is done quickly, and the cross is raised with one man at the base to guide the upright into the three-foot hole, while four other men raise the cross with braces pressing against the cross-member at the back, until the upright member seats in the hole. Two men then drive wedges down the insides of the hole to give the cross stability. This is done quickly, normally five minutes.

With the cross in place, the portion of the upright above ground is about eleven feet. The cross-member is attached about two feet from the top. This leaves the distance from the ground to the cross-member at nine feet.

Crucifixion crosses weigh about 130 pounds, give or take some, depending on whether the wood is green or seasoned.

Looking at the three crosses, I notice that the center one has an additional board nailed above the point where the victim's head would have been. It said:

Jesus of Nazareth, King of the Jews *

The identifying sign was an unusual feature. It was there by order of Pilate. He may have wanted to quell the demands of the prevailing establishment of Pharisees, and especially the Chief Priest and the Sanhedrin. The sign was to impress on them that this crucified man was indeed the man they wanted dead.

I can't look anymore. Sorrow weighs me down. The whole affair is gruesome. Ignoring Curtis, I turn and head back to Leah's, wondering if I'll have an appetite for supper. I feel so low.

By now, Ruth has given an account of what we saw and heard earlier at the crucifixion site. Leah and Reuben are astounded, but their knowledge of the master is based entirely on hear-say. I can see that they are impacted in a different way than I. I am morose. But they are only saddened and disgusted by the visible facts.

Their thoughts, even Ruth's, seem mundane to me. As we select food from the side-board (it's still Sabbath), they toss around

*** John 19:19**

questions such as: Why three victims? Why execute someone for thievery? Was the carpenter (their term) the first nailed? Why did he die before the thieves? Where are the thieves buried? Why did the Aramethean request the carpenter's body, but not the thieves bodies? Why did Pilate release the carpenter's body to a civilian (the execution was by Roman authority)? … and more.

My own thoughts are more focused: What will the master's followers and devotees do? What about the "twelve"? What about the master's personal friends; Mary Magdalene, Rebekah, and others? I keep my thoughts to myself.

The questions by the others go on and on as we take our supper selections to the table. We seat ourselves as before, with Ruth facing me. The questions and speculations continue. I remain mostly quiet. The others may assume that I am too shaken to talk. They are right.

Ruth and I make eye contact. She nods. I cough. It's settled. She wants to be free.

I break my silence to tell Leah and the others that I will be leaving early tomorrow for Nazareth.

I must give Rebekah a sad report.

CHAPTER X
ON THE BEACH!

WEALTH

The morning sky comes to life with crisp colors of pinks and reds. This may be a bad weather omen, but, not caring, I ride Hero out of Leah's stable with a purpose. The crucifixion was three days ago. The shock is easing a little, but I'm still utterly depressed. I need a change. I'm leaving very early. Jerusalem is still quiet.

Equipped with my sword and dagger, and a little food from Leah's sideboard, I'm hurrying to Nazareth, and thinking of Rebekah. She will be very sad about the crucifixion, and will mourn the master's death. But the thugs won't be back to bother her, and I need to tell her. That should temper the despair that she will surely feel over the master's death.

Fair weather seems to be holding. Pilgrims are streaming northward in scattered clusters, having departed the Passover celebration in Jerusalem. Bandits aren't likely to strike when such numbers are present, but I remain cautious.

Riding my sure-footed mule, I pass many walkers. Many are talking about the crucifixions. However, the significance of the master being one of the victims seems to have eluded them, so I assume that they are not devotees.

As I think about this, I conclude that most devotees of the master may be lingering in Jerusalem, too stunned to begin their long walks home.

I ride hard all day. Finally, toward the end of the day, the clusters of pilgrims thin out. Hero has carried me past most of them. Some may have dropped off already. Hero and I are both too tired to continue, so I decide to make a dry camp off the travel path.

We settle in a spot where I can be pretty sure of no bandits, and we'll take our chances on wild creatures. My travel pack contains a little water and grain, and just enough food to carry us through one more day.

I must have drifted into an exhausted sleep, for my next awareness was of morning sounds coming to life. My sister, Ruthie, now an adult, comes back to mind. I touch my pendant star and remember that Ruth is now a slave, and highly valued. How can I purchase her from Leah? This I don't know, but I know it's going to plague my thoughts.

My water supply is very low. I take a sip and give the rest to Hero along with a pint of oats. Hopefully, we'll find a well along the way. Gathering my gear, and reloading the lot on Hero's back behind the saddle, we return to the travel path which lays about a half mile west of our camp of last night.

Now, on our northbound journey to Nazareth, I see a few other travelers already on the path, some with donkeys. Not many have a horse or mule, much less a cart. Talk of the crucifixions still fills the air. Some are puzzled by the sign attached to one of the crosses, attesting that the victim was "King of the Jews."

When Ruth and I visited the site with Marco on the day after the crucifixions, Marco told me that the "king" identification was ordered by Pilate. Further, he said that Pilate tried to avoid sentencing the master, but finally yielded to the demands of the Chief Priest and the yelling mob of Pharisees. Otherwise, Pilate feared a riot.

Mulling these thoughts as I approach Nazareth, it occurs to me that a mob, or any crowd of emotional people, can become very cruel, and with very little reason. The anger seems to feed upon itself, and soar far higher than any one person, alone, would ever take it.

194

Mobs are dangerous. Even the smaller mob at the Nazareth synagogue, two years ago, grew from . . . intent to expel, to intent to kill . . . as their anger toward the master rose to fever pitch.

Looking beyond Hero's ears, I see Nazareth coming into sight. It's not yet mid-day. I go straight to Rebekah's house, tether Hero to a hitching rail, and go to the door. Peliel is there. We greet with a hug. "How's Rebekah," I ask. "She is doing well, and sleeping better now that my friend, Labon, and I watch over her and her property."

Peliel takes me in to see Rebekah. She is seated in her favorite chair. Her eyes light up as I enter the room, and she whoops a happy greeting. I kiss her cheek and tell her how well she looks (a bit of a stretch). She invites me to sit in the chair beside her. The chairs are large, making it easy for us to turn to face each other. She wants to know all about my trip. I tell her of the stressful time, and get right to the point.

When I tell her that our master was crucified, she breaks into sobs and weeps uncontrollably. I sit quietly. Finally, she gains control and asks for details.

Seeing that I'll be here a while, I ask Peliel to take Hero to the public stable, and request my friend, Rex, the stable master, to give him a rubdown and some oats and fresh hay.

After a pause, I begin telling Rebekah all I can about my last few days in Jerusalem. This leaves her terribly saddened. Sorrow seems to engulf her, and I cannot lift her spirits. When she falls to weeping from time to time, I just hold her hand.

Finally, I get the story told. She is crushed. She slumps in her chair.

As I rise to go, I tell her the thugs won't bother her anymore. They no longer have a reason.

I profess to be in a great hurry to get to Capernaum before dark, so I bid everyone shalom, and head to the stable.

Rex has treated Hero well, and he looks ready for the next ten miles, or so, to get us home. This stretch is uneventful. His stall in the stable, and my room in Tobias' inn, are welcome respites. I go to my room, collapse on my cot, and fall asleep.

At day-break I'm up and refreshed. Descending to the dining area, I find the cook has prepared a welcome dish of some kind of oat porridge, served with fruit and hot bread.

Tobias appears, and we talk most of the morning about my Jerusalem experience. He is loaded with questions. I give the facts. After that, we can only speculate.

In the back of my mind, I explore possible ways to gain Ruth's freedom, but I keep all of this to myself. If there is any hope at all, it will surely take money. But how much? That is the question.

Some gold is hidden in a secret compartment of my tool chest in the stable, but I need to add to it for sure. So, for the immediate future, I resolve to carve art and sell as much as I can, as quickly as I can, to build up my reserve. I need … *wealth!**

Tobias and I are still talking in the inn's common area when Danny rushes in.

Breathlessly, he shouts … NEWS! NEWS! BIG NEWS!

NEWS !!!

Danny shouts, "Travelers have entered the city telling a horrible tale! They are followers of the master! They say he was killed by crucifixion the day before the Sabbath!"

"Danny, it's true," I say. "I was there the next day. The cross was still standing. So were two other crosses, to execute thieves. The

*Author's note: It turns out that Ruth's ultimate pathway to freedom did not depend on Caleb's wealth.

God had other plans. More later.

196

Roman authorities ordered the executions, two apparently for thievery, and the other, the one for the master, for his alleged claim to be a 'king.' A sign on his cross declared him to be 'Jesus of Nazareth, King of the Jews!' It's true, Danny! What you heard is true!"

"But but but but" (Danny sounds like a flapping flag) "but but, . . . just listen to this! The day after Sabbath, they say his tomb was found *empty*!!! It had been closed tightly with a large rock, but when some women came to it with anointing spices, wondering who would open it for them, they found the tomb already open! And empty! This is what the latest travelers are saying!"

I can't believe it!! Could it be true?!

When I left Jerusalem a few days ago, my mule carried me the hundred miles north to Tobias' inn on the Sea of Galilee, with a brief stop in Nazareth. I was well ahead of the walkers who are just now arriving here in Capernaum. And if the walkers started later than I, they may have picked up news and rumors that I had totally missed.

"Danny, keep moving through the streets," I tell him, "and listen for anything related to the master's death. Meanwhile, I'll stay close to the inn, and try to engage incoming guests to learn more."

Chatting with Tobias, I wait for any guests traveling from Jerusalem. Eventually, two men arrive, brothers who've attended Passover in Jerusalem. And on their heels come three more, a man and two women. They have walked this far on the travel path.

The five were still full of talk. I quickly joined them in the common room, telling them what I had seen, and listening carefully to what they had to say. Whatever news we have is so new that it is still developing.

Later, alone, I try to separate the traveler's comments, and mine, into fact, hearsay, and questions. With what I already know, I finally settle on the following:

<u>Fact</u>
Three men were crucified; one being the master, the others being thieves.

A sign, in multiple languages, attached to the master's   cross, declared him to be "Jesus of Nazareth, King of the Jews." This by order of Pilate.

Many observers of the crucifixions were present, including family members.

The master's body was taken away by two of his followers and placed in a new tomb owned by Joseph of Arimathea.

By sundown, all bodies had been removed, but the crosses remained in place.

<u>Hearsay</u>
The thieves' bodies were probably destined for unmarked graves.

Most, but not all, of the master's core group (the Twelve) had scattered in fear.

One, the betrayer, returned the blood-money to the Chief Priest and, shortly after, he died either by accident or suicide, depending on the source.

The master's mother witnessed the executions. Mary of Magdala was also there. So was one of the bravest of the core group, John.

The master's tomb was identified, sealed, and guarded by Roman soldiers.
Three days after the crucifixion, some women went

to the tomb, found the sealing stone rolled away, leaving the tomb open and … empty.

Some are saying they have seen the master … alive.

<u>Questions</u>
Suppose the body was stolen. If so, by whom, and why? where is it? What about the guards? Have they been arrested? Or protected and secluded? (not likely)

The mystery of the guards' whereabouts is secondary to that of the master's body.

Or, did the master, dead and entombed, return to life?

The latter, astonishing as it is, just might be.

I need to know more about the rumors and the empty tomb. Mary of Magdala (Mary Magdalene) may know more. Riding Hero, I can be in Magdala in an hour or so. As you know, it's just down the shore a few miles from where we are now.

But night has fallen and this day is over. Early tomorrow, I'll head for Magdala.

EMPTY

The night seemed endless. I did not sleep well. Excitement and hope, and apprehension too, kept me in a restless state 'till dawn. But a quick breakfast and a jog to the stable restores my composure somewhat.

Hurriedly explaining to Boaz, the stable master, I saddle Hero and nudge him into a trot through the stable gate and down the slope to the Galilee shoreline. We start picking our way south, along the shore, toward Magdala. A mist, rising from the sea, makes for heavy fog and poor visibility, so Hero inches his way along the narrow overgrown foot path. For this short trip, the foot-path is more convenient than the more distant, wider travel path.

We stop often, listening in the silence. Any odd break in silence would alert my senses, but none has occurred so far. An hour passes before I reach the general area of the ramshackle shack from which I rescued Princess many weeks ago. I rein in my mule, and listen. No sounds of humans.

The fog has thinned a bit. Thick, thorny brush, stands between our path and the shack. I'm tempted to check the shack, but unwilling to delay my short journey any longer. So we push on toward Magdala.

Soon the sounds of chickens and dogs reach my ears, a promising sign that I'm approaching humans. Hero seems to sense the change too. He carries me on in his sure-footed way. It is mid-morning. The fog has lifted. The weather is nice now. A few people are in the open, attending to chores or errands.

Remembering the hospitality of Randy and Tabitha, I make my way to their home first. Remaining mounted, and holding Hero in place, I wait. Soon, we're noticed. Randy comes to the door and recognizes us immediately. He remembers my interest in the master from my last visit, and eagerly invites me in. I tether Hero and follow my friend.

Tabitha comes from the kitchen and greets me warmly. They ask if I'm selling carvings.

"No," I say, "but I'm hoping to get information about the Passover event in Jerusalem. Word is that your kinswoman, next door, was there. Maybe you were too. I was there myself, but left at daybreak after the Sabbath, earlier than most.

"Travelers stopping at the inn in Capernaum are telling astounding stories of the master's body disappearing. Some even say he's been seen alive. But this was after I left. So I'm looking for any trustworthy eyewitness reports of things that I missed."

Tabitha says "We weren't there this year, but my sister, Mary, was. She just returned yesterday, and she's been in a daze, trying to tell us of 'seeing' the master, but choking up in the effort."

Randy turns to his wife and asks, "Tabitha would you go next door to Mary's and invite her over? Tell her that Caleb's here." Within five minutes, the four of us are seated around Tabitha's kitchen table, leaning on our arms and elbows, as though trying to be closer to each other.

And we begin to talk! There is excitement and wonder in our voices! We're all talking, talking over each other. Until Randy slaps the table and brings us all to a halt. He says, "Let's do this one at a time until we've all had our say, then we can discuss our comments after they're all out in the open."

We all agree, and by common consent, I am first to tell what I know, but **only** what I know, **only** what I saw and heard with my own eyes and ears. I repeat the same facts that I gave to Tobias and Danny. I mention none of the hearsay at all.

Mary saw and heard much more, she says. She takes a deep breath, and begins:

"I saw the crucifixion from the beginning to the end. Hundreds had been drawn to the event. The crowd milled around until the crosses, with their victims nailed to them, were hoisted upright and eased into the holes that had been dug for them.

"We were in shock, especially those of us who knew and followed the master, Jesus. Most of the 'Twelve' had scattered for fear of arrest themselves. But Mary, the mother of the master, was there. She was being assisted and consoled as much as possible by John, one of the 'Twelve,' the bravest, judging by his presence. I saw none of the others. I know them all, and scanning the crowd, I saw only John, standing with the master's mother.

"I would have known if the others were there. The crucifixion lasted for hours, and I had plenty of time to look over the crowd. I did not see the master's siblings. Nor Joseph either. Word began circulating through the crowd that one of the Twelve was dead, either by accident or suicide, just that very day. His name was 'Judas.'

"Quite a number of people were at the crucifixion site. Of course, Roman soldiers were there to keep the peace and prevent any rescue attempts. But others were there too, most of whom I did not know. By their dress, I would say some were Pharisees, probably leaders of the synagogues, wanting to be certain that the master would indeed die. But the largest part of the crowd was the master's followers, most of whom were in shock.

"A sign over the master's head proclaimed him to be: 'Jesus of Nazareth, King of the Jews.' This was noted in three languages.

"Others in the crowd were just watchers, probably people who were simply in Jerusalem for the Passover observance. Pity was the prominent emotion of these.

"Among the devoted followers, some were clearly devoted to the master. I noticed a man from Arimathea who seldom left the foot of the master's cross. He had a companion, probably a friend. They stuck close together.

"One of my close friends, Mary by name ('Mary' is such a common name, I'll call her 'the other Mary'), stayed by my side. To make a distinction, I am usually called Mary Magdalene since my home is here in Magdala. 'The other Mary' and I only parted briefly at times when either of us searched for privacy to refresh ourselves.

"The victims sometimes spoke, but rarely. They spoke either to each other or to someone in the crowd. All utterances from the crosses were spoken in agony. Observers nearby were silent, listening for last words. More distant observers spoke in quiet tones.

"The master spoke to his mother, declaring one of the Twelve, John, to be her 'son.' And to John, standing beside her, he said 'behold your mother.'* John and the master's mother stood still, holding hands.

"In the outer depths of the crowd a murmur was constant but low-key, rising and falling, like gentle waves of the sea. Sometimes there would be a sharp short outcry from someone in the crowd, probably someone in despair.

"The guards, standing by, communicated with Pilate back at the Antonia Fortress, by runners. Two or three runners (young men) were always on hand. Late in the day, a runner raced from the Fortress to the chief guard with some sort of message.

"The message was evidently an order to hasten the victims' deaths, because the guards began breaking the shin bones of the victims. This resulted in a squeezing of the lungs, hastening death due to slumping of the bodies. But, looking at the master, one guard poked the sharp point of a spear in his side, and he did not flinch. At this, the guards must have concluded that he was already dead, so they did not bother to break his legs.

"'The other Mary' and I noticed at this point that the Arimathean spoke to the principal Roman guard. Almost immediately a runner was sent scampering to the Fortress. Within minutes, he, or maybe a relief runner, raced back to the guard with a message. Soon, thereafter, the Arimathean and his friend, with some help from the Romans, removed the master's body, and the two friends carried it away. 'The other Mary' and I followed.

"We saw the friends wrap the body, place it in a new tomb, seal the tomb with a large rock, and leave. Roman guards were stationed at the site to prevent any attempt to remove the body.

*John 19:26-27

They shooed us away. Our sorrow only worsened.

"'The other Mary' and I were guests of a friend in Jerusalem. We returned to her home just before sundown. Through the night, we each dealt with our sorrows alone.

But the next morning, a Sabbath, we found our voices and began discussing with each other our next moves."

* * *

This narration is interrupted when Randy calls for a quick break so everyone can stretch and refresh. Ten minutes later and we're back at the table, ready to resume. Randy asks Mary to continue. She begins again.

"'The other Mary' and I decided to visit the known 'haunts' of the Twelve (now reduced to eleven) to see if any of them had dared return to the city. Our host thought we were putting ourselves in danger by association, but we wanted to know what the Eleven planned to do, now that the master was dead. We quietly searched the city. After a few unproductive stops, we finally came to a home where the master had previously found friends. The eleven were huddled there.

"Fortunately, the owner recognized me as another 'friend of the master.' He said some of the Twelve were in a room upstairs, trying to stay off the streets and out of sight. But he thought they would like to see us.

"He led 'the other Mary' and me to the room, knocked on the door, and identified himself by voice. In a moment, the door slowly opened a crack, and we entered. The owner returned to his normal living quarters.

"Neither poet nor artist could have portrayed the sadness and despair in that room. Very little daylight seeped in. A lone candle burned on a small table in the center of the room. The air was rank with masculine sweat. Except for the one who let us enter, all were slumped on the floor, their backs to the wall. Two or three held their heads and sobbed in occasional muted bursts.

"They knew us. For at least two years, we had occasionally been with the master and the Twelve. Along with others, we sometimes provided food and money, brought news, took and delivered messages, and gave general assistance. Judas always handled the money.

"But now, in the dimness of the room, despondency was in the air. Someone moaned, 'the master is dead.' Another said, 'Judas too.' Still another voice said, 'traitor.' Then the room fell silent again . . .until someone said, 'It's over.' Another said, 'We need to regroup.' But then the voices became quiet again.

"We told the miserable Eleven that we would visit the tomb the next morning, the first day after the Sabbath. No one spoke. As we eased the door open to leave, someone thanked us for coming. We found the home owner, and visited briefly before taking our leave. All we could do then was to wait out the Sabbath. No spice markets were open.

"But next morning, 'the other Mary' and I bought burial spices as soon as shops opened. We set out for the tomb, wondering if any capable men would be on hand to roll the sealing stone away for us. We weren't sure that we could persuade the authorities even to open it. But we intended to try.

"As we approached the site from some two hundred yards away, something didn't look right. We saw no guards. We were hoping the expected guards would honor our intentions and open the tomb for us. But where were the guards, we wondered? Getting closer, we could see the stone was already moved. But why? And, by whom? Still no guards.

"The gaping hole was wide open. A weak ray of daylight revealed a bare slab, but no body! Just a linen cloth, folded!

"We stood at the opening, looking in. Walking around the area,

I saw a man that I took to be the gardener of the grounds. 'Sir,' I said, 'the body is missing from this tomb. Where is it?'

"The man looked at me, and said, **'Mary.'** The voice was unmistakable. The figure, too. I knew it was the master! I fell to my knees, and said, 'Teacher!' He said, **'Don't touch me.' Go tell the Eleven to take heart.'** *

"I raced back to the Eleven with the news! In so many words, they all said, 'It can't be!' But Peter and John bolted from the room, raced to the tomb, and saw it empty! They ran back to the others and confirmed that the tomb is empty!

"But … where is the master?

"Could he really be alive?!!

"Confused, the Eleven resumed their place in the hideout.

"They do not know what to do."

* * * * *

After hearing Mary's account, we linger around Randy's table, talking for hours. We finally decide that we'll stay alert for any other reliable news, and meet again soon.

Hero and I begin our return to Capernaum, only a few miles.

ALIVE !

Back at the inn, in the privacy of my room, I try to pull together what we know.

Mary Magdalene saw the master … back from the dead … alive! … in the garden beside the tomb! She is absolutely certain! She

*** John 20:17**

has no doubt! She knows the master very well, and cannot be mistaken!

Later, on the same day that Mary Magdalene had seen the living master, she visited the despondent Eleven in their hideout.

The Eleven didn't believe her, but shortly after she left them, they saw the master too, right there in the hideout. He didn't enter through the door; he was just there. He talked with the Eleven, and then vanished as quickly as he had appeared.

At that point, one of the Eleven rushed out to find this same Mary who had just visited them. He told her what happened.

This is what he told her: Jesus suddenly appeared to them in their "secret" room. They did not have to open the door. In an instant, he was there. How he entered, they do not know. He just appeared. Instantly! And they spoke with him, and he with them. And then, just as quickly, he was gone.*

It was then that the Eleven bounded out of their hiding place, into the open. Courage returned. They remembered the master's teachings, that he was indeed the "sacrificial lamb" that John the baptizer had proclaimed.

Mary Magdalene learned these things from one of the disciples, but she soon heard even more from others!

She said some of the general public began to see him too. They saw him within the city as well as on the byways. Some exchanged greetings and comments with him, and ate with him. This was unheard of: resurrection, not by power of any man, nor by self-will, but by the power of God, the Creator.

Mary gained these updates from her occasional encounters with some of the disciples, primarily those of Galilee, as well as some of the master's many other devotees.

*** Based on Luke 24:36-39**

Mary's hometown of Magdala, you may recall, like mine, is on the shore of the Sea of Galilee.

Word is rapidly spreading that the man from Nazareth, crucified only days ago, is alive and circulating. I'm hearing it nearly every day, much of it from travelers stopping in at Tobias' inn.

But I really want super solid proof. I want to see with my own eyes. To that end, I decide to go to places where he used to be found talking to crowds of people. It's my best chance of a sighting.

Back on the shore of the Sea of Galilee, I roam among the fishermen, day after day.

I see only the "regulars" among the fishermen, until, one day, I spot James, one of the sons of Zebedee.

James is one of the original Twelve (now Eleven). The master is leaving his disciples on their own for a time, he says. Some are visiting their home areas. Some have returned to Galilee, and resumed their former occupation as fishermen.

But the master told the Eleven to reconvene in Jerusalem, says James, and wait for a great happening. The mystery of this command is sure to get them there. So, no matter where the Eleven are at this moment, they will soon be in Jerusalem.

Today, I search out my old fisherman friend, Ramon. He and I are strolling along the shore of the Sea of Galilee in the early dawn, reminiscing over the last few years; the storm, and the resulting loss of his fishing boat, and his near death in the event, his dog, finding the little girl, Princess, and more. It's early morning. The sun is just rising above the horizon. It's rays caress the earth with soft shifting colors accented by patches of fog.

Suddenly we stop in our tracks, Ramon and I. We gaze ahead!

We **see** him! We stand as still as stumps, silent in awe!

We take in the scene. Down the shore a way, we see a small fire of hot coals and fish roasting on sturdy sticks. A few men are hunkered there, eating. Ramon and I recognize the men, some of the Eleven, natives of Galilee. And there is the other. We recognize him, and speak in unison … *"the master!!"*

It is the master!! No doubt about it. Eating roasted fish with some of the Eleven. There is Peter and Andrew! John, too! And a few others! **(Based on John 21:9-14)**

At last, I see him with my own eyes! So does Ramon! He is … *alive!! Jesus of Nazareth … the Messiah!*

Now we know! Isaiah's prophesies, read by Jesus in the Nazarene synagogue nearly three years ago have come true:

Jesus of Nazareth *is the Messiah!*

alive today, and forever.

CHAPTER XI
FORTY YEARS LATER

CALEB'S MINISTRY AND MISSION

It's time to return my thoughts once again to the present.

* * * * * *

Forty years have passed since my old fisherman friend, Ramon, and I last saw Jesus. In that instance, we saw him and some of his disciples roasting and eating fish on the shore of the Sea of Galilee. We were astounded to see Jesus alive!

Only days before, Jesus had been crucified, and his dead body entombed. But now, Jesus was alive! I saw him! Ramon did too.

Others also reported seeing him, not only in Galilee, but even more in and around Jerusalem some ninety miles to the south where the crucifixion took place. Some had met him and ate with him.

So, it was obvious that Jesus was alive. Reports that he returned to life three days after his death were clearly true.

Weeks later, some of his disciples reported witnessing Jesus ascend heavenward. Jesus told them he was going to God, his Father. But he promised to return someday, maybe in our day, or maybe a future day.

And we are to watch for him.

Much has happened in the forty years since the "ascension" of Jesus. For one thing, I've been blessed with wealth through my art. My engravings are so popular that I've established an art colony where apprentices multiply my output many times over. This art has continued selling year after year, far and wide, bringing a growing wealth.

As my wealth grows, I gradually buy property for the purpose of advancing the teachings of Jesus. I've already bought the inn on the Sea of Galilee, and then the city stable near it, and finally hundreds of acres of farm land just outside of Capernaum.

The centerpiece of my "ministry" (I called it that from the start) is the inn, now enlarged, and surrounded by several other structures.

I named the compound THE ISLE OF HOPE, and dedicated it, in the name of Jesus, to the needs of those the master spoke of in the Nazareth synagogue and elsewhere so long ago.

They were:

the poor:	those impoverished, hungry,or homeless
the imprisoned:	by addiction, fear, jail
the impaired:	those lame, mental, blind
the oppressed:	those abused, mocked, hated
the abandoned:	the outcast, ignored, shunned

THE ISLE OF HOPE

The Isle of Hope is served by an extensive staff, providing help for those unfortunate people burdened by one or more of the afflictions just mentioned, those outlined by Jesus in the Nazarene synagogue and throughout his days on Earth.

"Residents" of the Isle of Hope, as they are able, are given tasks in the compound (some on the farm, some in grain millage and storage, some in craft work, some in foodservice, some in maintenance, some in nursing, etc.).

The main building (the former inn), together with it's satellite buildings, can accommodate about 300 "residents." A few are permanent, but most are temporary until they can re-enter society in a positive way.

All of these residents and staff are fed and clothed by output from the surrounding farms (part of the ministry). Surplus farm products generate more than enough cash to support the Isle of Hope. There is no cost to any resident.

The guiding motto of the Isle of Hope, expressed by Jesus himself is:

"Love God, and love one another"

Author's note: The Isle of Hope is idealistic, made to support the story of Caleb. Its existence is only in the mind of the author.

And a few more notes by the author:

FICTIONAL CHARACTERS
OF THE STORY

CALEB AND RUTH

An aging Caleb occupies one small suite in the main building (former inn), of The Isle of Hope. He never married, but his sister, Ruth, did. Ruth married Caleb's very close friend, Reuben.

Ruth was freed from slavery by Leah as a wedding gift when Ruth married Reuben (Leah's son). Reuben was finally recognized for his intelligence and management skill. He and Ruth occupy a second suite in the main building. Reuben has trained a team of young managers to administer all divisions of the Isle of Hope.

212

Ruth, Reuben, and Caleb, remain solid friends to this day.

Reuben is in his eighties and Ruth is in her seventies. They have two children, now workers on the farm which is part of the Isle of Hope complex.

These children, now adults, are training to become the next generation general managers of the Isle of Hope.

* * * * * *

OTHER FICTIONAL CHARACTERS

Parents of Caleb and Ruth; enslaved, likely dead.

Dan and Leah, parents of Reuben. Deceased. Buried near Jerusalem.

Nathan. Seafaring brother of Reuben: retired to Crete.

Tobias the innkeeper. Deceased. No surviving family. No heirs.

Boaz the stable master, died while working in the stable. Buried nearby.

Hero, Caleb's mule, buried near the city stable.

Rebekah, mourned the death of the master, but never saw him alive again. Deceased.

No-name (Newman) died an old man at the height of his popularity.

Ike, fugitive killer, was himself killed by fellow beggars.

Zeb and Leah of the Jericho Road, grew feeble, died in their son's home.

Ramon, became old, was lost at sea, never found.

The girl named Princess, married Danny, Caleb's young assistant.

Marco, dropped from sight after the crucifixion of Jesus.

And then there are these:

(True characters)

Jesus returned to God, his Heavenly Father.

John the baptizer was executed by Herod.

Herod, died, haunted by the memory of John the baptizer.

Pontius Pilate was recalled to Rome, died a suicide, according to some sources.

Judas, entered history as a traitor, dying by suicide or accident, depending on sources.

Matthias replaced Judas among the Apostles.

The Twelve (now including Matthias) became evangelists, some were murdered for the sake of Jesus.

Mary Magdalene, no further record.

FINALLY

Saul of Tarsus, a Pharisee, tried to crush the Jesus movement, but was converted and re-named Paul the Apostle of Jesus Christ. For the rest of his life he worked to promote and establish Christian churches throughout the Mediterranean world. *

*** See Acts 9:1-19**

About The Author

Eugene Wesley Vest was born to Clarice and Cody Vest on June 26, 1935, in a modest mountain home near Hinton, WV. A year later, in 1936, the Vests moved to Maxwelton, WV and opened a "mom and pop" general store in which Eugene (Gene) was allowed to roam freely as a very young preschooler. One or sometimes both of Gene's parents were always present to watch over him.

Gene was fascinated by a certain set of local customers who would habitually loaf at the store and speak their minds with whomever might come by. And they would talk and laugh, sometimes loudly, sometimes softly, about most anything: the weather, the hay crop, a sick cow, politics, other people, or maybe neighbors, and always about hunting. This lingers in Gene's memory of country living in the late 30s, and remains a part of his education to this day.

The Vest family was rounded out in the 40s with the births of Gene's sisters, Mary and Georgia. The three siblings were raised by their Christian parents, and all three became professing Christians before they left the comfort of home. The three graduated from different colleges, became professionals, and raised Christian families of their own.

Gene earned BS and MS degrees in Mechanical Engineering, and worked primarily as an engineer or teacher until he retired.

Over the years, Gene has been active in Church life, serving in several Christian denominations as he moved from place to place. He embraces Jesus' summation of the law: "Love the Lord your God with all your heart, mind, soul, and strength, and love your neighbor as yourself."

Gene treasures the unexpected urging by a beloved uncle, Willard Hedrick, just days before his uncle died at the age of ninety: "Believe on the Lord Jesus Christ and you shall be saved."

Gene and his first wife, Roberta, (deceased) are the parents of four children, followed by nine grandchildren and twelve great-grandchildren.

Gene and his wife, Nan, reside in Florida.